Christopher Blehm

17 JUNE 11

Descanse

For Dad

Who, on top of everything else,
taught me to relax and concentrate.

CONTENTS

Mercy of the Elements

Mercy

When Mercy raised the tequila to her lips, she caught the smell of blood on her fingers. She threw back the glass anyway, licking salt and ocean and still more salt down with the fire. The salt in the auburn hair that just brushed her shoulders was not from the shot glass, but perhaps the deepening of her sea grey eyes was. Losing a job was as good an excuse as any, much like the free drinks she usually still enjoyed, depending on the bar. This one, the Marlin Club, was shaped like a boat, the stern butting into the back wall, lined with bottles and curving to a graceful, proper prow, complete with mermaid. False portholes peered out from between barstools, and the worn, brown bar top heaved slowly from side to side, at least for some of the patrons. The bartender stood in the ship's interior, shuffling drinks and pulling cash from the forlorn souls adrift in the sea, clinging to her sides by their elbows. It was a proper island bar, dark and dank and a stone's throw from the temperate Pacific. In the far corner fishermen sat lying, the palms of their upheld arms spreading farther apart with each beer. At the pool table two blonde college girls on vacation were circled by six or seven college boys. The pinball game was broken, but the perfect height for the third college girl to sit upon and be groped by the tallest of the boys.

Mercy knocked the empty shot glass twice on the bar, once for thanks towards the elbow of the regular who had bought it for her, and once to the rotund bartender for another. She nursed a beer for economy's sake. The grizzled fixture across from her neither expected nor desired conversation over the shot. He pushed his glass back and went outside to smoke alone in the fading light. She paid for the next tequila herself, and tipped generously, for economy's sake. Like most all bartenders this one was fat and jovial and his eyes had the look of longing for the other side of the bar. To distract himself he cleaned incessantly with a small white towel and made small talk with anyone tipping, anyone cute. He watched the legs of the pinball game for signs of weakening.

"Why'd Lucky Tom fire you?"

"Because I wouldn't sleep with him," she said as she slid the second empty shot glass over to him with the bottom of her beer bottle.

"You've worked there more than two years."

"And I didn't sleep with him," she insisted.

"So why'd he fire you today?"

"Because I wouldn't sleep with him."

"Bullshit. How'd you get blood on your hands?"

"There isn't any blood on my hands," she said, looking again to make sure she was right.

"I can smell it. You can wash the red off, but not the stink."

"What's the difference?"

"Nothin'. You want to sleep with me?"

"Hell, no."

"Well, then, I guess you're fired," he said, and went back to watching the pinball game.

Mercy chuckled as she pursed her lips and raised her bottle for another sip. Her stomach felt fine now, none of the rumblings from this afternoon, none of the knotting as she dug her money from her pockets on the way to the bar. Soon one of the college kids sat next to her, brushing his curly blonde locks out of his boyish, bloodshot eyes as they roamed over her. Another shot glass appeared in her hand, this one she sipped as she listened to him talk of school and his frustration with "women" his age. She noticed that his watch was worth more than her dive gear, all of it.

"I have a boat, you know," he bragged. She wished he wouldn't speak; he really was kind of cute when he was silent.

"Really? Is it here?"

"Yeah, out in the father, I mean, out in the harbor." He was slurring only slightly and forging boldly on, aware of his friend's eyes on his back, except for the one already engaged in pinball.

"How long are you guys staying?"

"We sail back to the Point in a couple of days, probably..." he trailed off.

"What?"

"You, you want to see it?" he prepared to scurry back to his comrades as soon as she said no, and she shocked them both by saying yes.

He didn't try to hold her hand on the way down the green pier, and he was smooth and accomplished in starting the outboard on the small white inflatable and casting off from the dinghy dock. As he steered past the moorings and towards the deeper anchorages for the big boats, Mercy sat on the bow and thought about all that had occurred that morning.

-

She awoke before dawn on the dive boat and had the heads cleaned by the time the sun peeked above the low line of fog ghosting over the ocean. During multiday trips it was both home and workplace. Then the galley and still she was the only one awake. The diving gear and fishing poles and spear guns were rinsed yesterday evening, before the salt could dry and cake and interfere. The back deck needed no cleaning; it had not been stained since the trip began three days ago. They would dock and offload this afternoon, and she could clean it then. Her chores finished, she waited for the captain and crew to wake and relieve her. She could then sleep until the first dive, and then help with the heavy tanks and tangled lines and share in the tips.

She heard it before she saw it, a gurgling rush of froth and bubbles just to stern. She slipped to the back of the boat and saw the boil, a churning mass of water and fish and soon thereafter birds. Small silver baitfish fluttered to the surface by the thousands, frantic for any escape from the school of yellowtail attacking them from below. The school was large, dozens of shiny black and white sides driven by yellow scythe like tails. Some of the fish weighed forty pounds. They surrounded the bait ball, turning in an instinctual circle, driving the mackerel and top smelt into a tight knot, then charging in and feeding and returning to circle. When the gulls overhead noticed they began diving, pulling the bait from the water and flying away from the boil to land and bob and swallow. It might last for an hour, or be over in an instant. The frenzied mass migrated slowly to port, and began to drift away from the anchored boat.

Mercy pulled a mask and fins from the storage bin, and then a spear gun from the fly deck. It was a simple thing, a five foot long wooden stock grooved to hold a steel shaft and three stout lengths of rubber tubing – a huge underwater rubber band gun. The shaft attached to the gun with a thin steel cable, so it would hold a fish and not be lost, and from the butt of the gun a line trailed some fifty feet to a float. She pulled off her t-shirt, not bothering with a wetsuit, and plunged in. The icy current rushed through her, hardening her nipples and making her breath hitch in her throat.

-

He lifted his mouth from her breast, panting, and centered his hard weight on top of her. She arched her back for him, offering the other firm, reddening button to his tongue. He smelled of beer and smoke and young sweat, and she could feel the boat move beneath her despite its size. He was lost in his haze and fevered delirium and she drifted back to the hunt.

-

She calmed herself on the surface, and lodged the butt of the gun in her hip, where her leg met her torso. Then she reached forward, grasping one of the surgical tubes and drawing it back towards her, arms straining in the cold water. She pulled harder and harder still, finally slipping the thin line at the base of the tube over a notch in the spear. The other two were easier, and as she loaded the bands she felt the gun come alive and coil, ready to strike. She flipped the safety lever and began to swim. The school remained hidden in the gloom as she kicked silently towards it. Thirty feet away she took two long, deep breaths, and slipped beneath the surface. She had no weight belt to aid her descent, and was forced to kick. She leveled off beneath the waves and saw only dark water. Then, suddenly, baitfish began flying past in an insane silver snowstorm. She was blinded and one thumped off the glass of her mask, forcing bubbles out the top. She was twenty feet below the surface, the pressure a gentle push on her lungs and then the bait was gone and there was nothing but blue and black and silence save her heart in her ears.

-

He was naked now and she watched his pale rear bob in the darkness of the cabin as he groped through his drawers and luggage. She could see the length of him when he turned sideways to search another bag, long and stiff and swaying with his movements. She reached out and grasped him, drew him to the bunk, pushed him onto his back, and began a slow, rhythmic stroke ending in a twist that made him moan. She grasped him tighter, seeing him swell even in shadow, and then released and twisted again, feeling him fight uselessly against his youth.

-

First there was one and then another and then the school surrounded her. The fish cruised past effortlessly, eyeing her with vast black orbs and streaked with color from their excitement. The silver sides ebbed greens and purples as they pulsed into the current, following the bait. Mercy raised the gun and swung it across the current, trailing and tracking through the fish closest to her. She forced herself to raise the spear tip, higher and higher still, knowing the tremendous effect of water and gravity on trajectory. She swung the tip high and past the fish, and in one fluid pull released the spear ahead of its path. It swam inevitably forward as the spear sped and dropped and plunged into its side. The gun came alive in her hands as the fish exploded, writhing and fighting. She grabbed the line and kicked to the surface. She pulled, feeling the strong, instinctual, futile struggle at the other end. Soon the spear was in her right hand and then her left found the gills and she began the pull back to the boat, trailing blood in the water.

She stood quietly, regaining her breath, regaining her heat, the smell beginning to rise from her hands. She pulled her shirt back on, watching him quiver and then fall silent.

The Tsunami and the Wall

While the young man slept, the blood of a four hundred year old curse stirred on the other side of the world, and changed it forever as it woke. Buildings swayed in Tokyo, and panicked millions rushed into the streets, but the earthquake was merely the prologue. The resultant tsunami lashed the island nation with a force unimaginable. It killed tens of thousands. It carried a two thousand ton ship over a mile inland and dropped it on a house, killing everyone inside. It ruptured nuclear reactors and reawakened the greatest Japanese fear of all. It also managed to hit Mercy's cousin right square in the ass.

Her cousin used to live near the beach outside Sendai, and what had once been his house was reduced to dripping rubble months after he moved to China. Nevertheless, the tsunami still managed to hit him in the ass. While Mercy watched the boy sleep, her cousin was walking down the beach past the land he used to buy and sell. He held his new Chinese wife by the hand and she held the wrist of their child toddling his long bones and jet black hair. They were fresh off the plane from Shanghai, enjoying his old stomping grounds and new family. Everybody, Mercy included, thought they were safe in China, miles from the danger. They were walking right into it.

As they strolled down the beach, suddenly there came a strange sucking sound, and in an eerie creep the water began to recede. As passers by stopped to gaze in disbelief, that old prelude to fear, the water withdrew further and further from shore. After a few moments it had withdrawn far enough to expose scores of paces of the bottom. People began to wander tentatively out as crabs scuttled after the foam and fish flipped in disbelief on the new sand.

Her cousin froze in realization and looked at the waterline receding far into the sea, and as he later said in a mildly sarcastic academic tone that would one day make him rich, "I did the fucking math." He thrust his first and only child into his wife's arms and shouted at her to run, run up the hill, run.

His wife disappeared up the slope, dragging their child and then lifting him, running towards the glass-walled hotel that once made him enough money to leave Sendai for the booming economy in China, and he started to second guess himself. Not about China, but about his fear, and was it panic, and why was his wife the only one running? Was this an annual tide festival and was he going to look like an ass? And then he heard it, and a moment later others did too.

It started as a gentle reversal of the flow that had pulled the water away, and preceded itself with a temperate wall of wind. Then the width and breadth and mass of the blue gave way to gravity and surged back towards shore, driven by an angry earth breaking free deep beneath the waves and the sea floor. He turned and ran as the sound hibernated briefly and reawakened in a roar. Others behind him began to flee; he could hear the wet klop-suck of their heels in the clay and sand of the shore. His loafers weren't built for sprinting, but they didn't seem to care as they hit the blacktop at the edge of the beach, outside the hotel. He slapped ran to the doors and made the entrance and was halfway to the stairs when the wave hit the glass of the front lobby.

The stairwell receded before him, much as the water had before, and he was sucked into the terror of that universal dream of running in slow motion. He remembered the sound of shattering glass and the sound of screams but not which came first. He said it didn't matter much, but it still bothered Mercy.

He thought he was never going to reach the stairwell and the water proved him wrong. As he later said it to Mercy, the tsunami hit him right square in the ass, knocked him off his feet and onto it, and slammed him into the staircase he had wanted in the first place. The froth drilled him into the wall, thankfully feet first, and he rebounded and rode the wave up. Problem is, as anyone who's been in a staircase can visualize, that tall ones double back twice every story, and it became necessary to negotiate a 180 to prevent drowning against the ceiling.

That is precisely what Mercy's cousin was forced to do, dazed and on his back and thankfully buoyed up by his fear-filled lungs. He crawled across the ceiling of the abandoned staircase as the flood pressed harder from below, reducing his atmosphere to a sliver between the stairs. He made the landing of the second floor and gasped in fresh lungfulls as the water pushed him higher still, though slower now. It stopped when he was even with the banister at the top of the second level, and he managed to grab the trembling steel with both hands before the water fell away from his body, taking his shoes and one sock, leaving him dangling in space.

He heaved himself up and over the railing almost effortlessly, adrenaline mocking that small feat next to what he had just endured. It was further fueled by the possibility of the wave returning, and it did for some, though not nearly so high as he had been driven. He made the roof and searched for his wife and son. It took him about ten minutes, or as he described it, a century, to find her on the roof, son clutched to her breast, near hysteria as she had known he was behind her when the wave hit. They caught each other in their arms and he caught his breath and they began to survey the carnage visible below from their perch on the roof. Dozens more milled about, and they watched some reunite, and others become increasingly frightened that they never would.

Hours later and half a world away, on the opposite side of the Pacific, the last geodesic tremors and oceanic surges swirled around Santa Catalina Island, some twenty six miles across the sea from Southern California. Waves surged into Cat Harbor on the back side of the island, capsizing small skiffs and pushing an empty barge across the bay, but causing no injuries. On the front side of the island, it wasn't enough to be felt by anything except dogs, cats, and seismographic buoys, and then was little more than a tickle. The boy didn't even wake up. Mercy was on the phone with her cousin, confirming his safety and listening to his agony as he described the devastation around him. As they talked, the last tremor of the tsunami clipped a pinnacle known as Ship Rock just off the northwest edge of Catalina, and started a small underwater land slide. It was nothing like the massive earthquake that began the whole mess, merely a tired patch of slope sliding gently from the shallows into the deep. What remained behind was a new wall, topping out some sixty feet from the surface, terracing briefly at a hundred twenty feet before plunging into the deep. It was a new face in the abyss, and as the sand slid away it revealed a glint of metal that no one had seen for four centuries.

4th November 1587 and the Months Before

A year and a half of waiting on the water was over. A Spanish sail shone on the horizon and underneath it treasure. The English Captain Edmund Oswald had been patient, evident in the worn wood of the helm he held for many leagues. Both voyage and patience were sustained by blood. Tonight it would be sauce for the gold.

-

Four months earlier the English Admiral Thomas Cavendish captured a Spanish messenger ship dispatched from Rio Dolce. From it he learned of the impending arrival of the Spanish galleon from Manila, precisely because the messenger bark carried a warning to the galleon of the English. The Englishman found this delightful. Edmund had stood off in his smaller ship, the *Content,* while Admiral Cavendish steered the *Desire* alongside and seized the Spanish bark and all aboard her.

Among the captured crew was a French sailor named Michael Sancius. He told the Admiral in a muddle of broken English and loudly repeated French about the galleon, and his orders to alert her to the presence of the English pirates. The Admiral resented the degradation of "pirate," and cuffed the Frenchman about the perimeter of the Captain's quarters, proclaiming a mission of the Crown. Then he held Sancius captive and sailed for the southern tip of the land called California, later named Cabo San Lucas. The hunt for the galleon was on.

The two ship flotilla arrived on the 14th of October and spent the next month patrolling the point, eyes to sea, waiting. Their prize would be laden with all the wonder of the Philippines and the south sea, gold and silver and silk and spices. It was to be carried to Acapulco, loaded onto mule trains for the trip across the narrow tip of Southern Mexico, and then onto another Galleon at Vera Cruz for the treacherous voyage through the Caribbean and to Spain. A fifth of it was guaranteed to the King, which is why such a small portion of what was actually on board any Spanish galleon was ever officially declared.

Cavendish and Edmund had other plans for the treasure. The Admiral interrogated the Frenchman and goaded his English crew with the promise of gold for the first to sight their prey, and rivers more of it for every man who helped capture her.

-

Edmund's head snapped about when he heard the trumpeter's cry, and "Sail, ho!" still echoed off the creaking planks when he spotted her and began to twist and squeeze the helm again. He followed the Admiral's ship in a tight turn, sails swinging about on their booms, while the Englishmen shouted and shoved ordinance into place. And they gained on the galleon, side by side, Cavendish and Edmund, *Desire* and *Content*.

-

The past year was not without pleasure for Edmund. Though captain of the smaller ship, he enjoyed considerable leeway when leading raiding parties on shore or the occasional boarding party swarming over a captured

16

ship at sea. Admiral Cavendish thought himself a gentleman, and therefore found it unseemly to commit acts of questionable character in front of the men – men Edmund knew were only too willing to play along.

True, they had marauded through a North African seaside town in Sierra Leone, their first landfall since departing Plymouth. That night they befriended the natives, dancing around fires and feasting. Their bona fide intention was to reconnoiter a Portuguese vessel already anchored in the harbor. Cavendish wanted her and Edmund was tempted by the possibility of what she held. In the end the Admiral called off the attack plans, proclaiming the risk too great and the chances of real treasure too small. Edmund was not so sure they defined it the same way. The next day he returned with a landing party of seventy men and attacked his dance partners from the night before. They fled into the jungle and Edmund plundered and then burned the town when he found nothing of value. As he swept back to the beach and the stout long boat, the natives returned behind a rain of poison arrows. Men cried out and one succumbed days later. Some of the captured blacks, men and women, were brought on board both boats to man the pumps or vice versa. What would dear Cavendish do when the inevitable pregnancies began to show? But there had been no treasure. Not in Sierra Leone and not since.

-

Edmund saw the signal man's cloth wave on board the *Desire* and he pushed the rudder slightly, putting more crystalline water between the *Content* and her flagship. The approach would be similar to the one they used to capture the bark carrying the news of this galleon, though the prey far larger. Manila Galleons displaced upwards of 700 tons, and would only grow larger over the next two centuries. The *Desire* was 120 tons, the *Content* but 60. Cavendish would sweep alongside the much larger and slower ship, sending a boarding party over the rails. Perhaps they could take her with only a brief struggle. The Spanish considered the Pacific their private lake, and despite Sir Francis Drake's triumphant, bloody course around the globe nine years earlier, they feared no attack in their new backyard. Some galleons carried cannon, other times they were offloaded in Manila to "aid in the defense of the settlements," which sounded, particularly to the conquering Spanish ear, like "make room for more treasure." While Cavendish and the *Desire* attempted to subdue the prize, Edmund would hold the *Content* nearly even, but slightly aft and to port some distance. If it became necessary for the Admiral to loose the *Desire's* cannons, Edmund did not want to be along the far side of the Spanish ship.

They gained on her. Edmund could see the outline of wood beneath the ever growing smudge of white that were her sails. He put more distance between the *Content* and the *Desire* and ordered a bit of sail dropped, holding back, for the time being.

After Sierra Leone they cut southwest across the Atlantic, making landfall on the coast of South America at 48° S. Cavendish named the harbor Port Desire and they went ashore on the 17th of December. They replenished their depleted meat lockers with sea lion and penguin, and beached the boats one at a time to careen them and scrape the thick growth from the bottoms. The strange creatures and clinging plant life debilitated a ship's speed, and the worms destroyed the wooden planks if left unchecked.

A man and boy, while doing their laundry, were lost to an ambush, and the ships were refloated and guarded more closely thereafter. The failed search party returned with nothing save a scrap of shirt and tales of footprints eighteen inches long.

They left Port Desire on the 28th of December and entered the Strait of Magellan just after celebrating the new year. To date, only two men's expeditions had succeed in circumnavigating – Magellan's and Drake's, Magellan albeit personally finishing his voyage rotting in a box after dying under the steel of Philippine warriors. He had discovered the passage between the main land mass of South America and the substantial Tierra del Fuego, and led his crew into the south seas and Asia. When Drake followed Magellan's course he navigated the dangerous strait only to emerge into the very teeth of a Southern Pacific storm. He was blown southeast all the way past Cape Horn. Thus the Cape, the most treacherous passage on the planet, was discovered from behind. Cavendish intended to avoid Cape Horn, follow Magellan's path through the strait, and sail up the western coast of the Americas, burning everything Spanish in his path and seizing all his two ships could hold and any they could capture and crew before taking the long way home.

-

The closing speed faltered when the Spaniards recognized them not as sister ship and bark, which they had undoubtedly hoped, but the English aggressors they were. When they turned and ran, Cavendish acknowledged their flight by raising the red and white of England in defiance and threat. Everyone on that small stretch of sea that day knew whose ships were faster. Edmund kept up with the *Desire* easily, and his men began to grow restless, realizing that once again they would not be in front for the fight. His navigator and second in command, a tall, thin, angled package of a man trussed in naval blue, came to the helm and reported their position.

"She is making for the coast, hoping to land in a port that can protect her from us," he told his navigator while gesturing to the horizon.

"She doesn't stand a chance in hell."

"Perhaps they know that, but they run anyway."

"It gives them time to prepare to fight," the Navigator said.

"I hope so."

Hamdullah

When Mercy slid onto the stool next to him his eyes said nothing of the night before. The fat bartender asked if her boy toy had sailed home and slopped beer foam on her napkin when he plunked down a draught. She didn't mention that she was taking the young man diving the next morning.

She had seen the grizzled old salt on the same perch at the Marlin Club every day for a year. And the one before that, as well, she thought as she pondered his elbow, expecting it to leave an impression in the wood when he raised it to drink. They called him that – Elbows. He might have been forty-five or sixty, though lean, not smooth. He cradled a bottle of banquet beer in his right hand and gazed at its shot glass sidekick.

"So you looking for work, Mercy?"

"No, he hired me back," she replied. The bartender lumbered closer and said, "Why, did you sleep with him too?" He turned to cleaning when the hand holding the shot glass leveled a finger at him.

"Why did he hire you back?"

"The same reasons he hired me in the first place," she supposed as she sipped.

"And why was that, my dear?" Elbows persisted.

"My experience, and the fact that he needs somebody."

"That is certainly true."

"Up yours, Elbows. I'm remembering why I don't talk to you anymore."

"How can you know why you stopped doing something you've never done?"

"Up yours, Elbows."

"Just look me in the eye and tell me your looks have nothing to do with -"

"Elbows, at my age looks are good for about a weekend. And underwater they're good for as long as you can hold your breath."

"I've known girls quite a bit older than you that've gotten by on their looks. Some of 'em their whole lives."

"I notice you don't spend much time with them."

"I'm not sure where they are." They both chuckled and drank.

"He liked your experience?" Elbows offered without turning his head.

"Yeah, I've worked all over the Caribbean. Nassau, the Caymans, I wanted to go to Belize but it didn't happen."

"I dived Sharm-el-Sheikh for a year." Mercy turned towards Elbows, surprised at the unusual invitation to openness. She decided to reply elegantly.

"No shit."

"None."

"How the hell did you end up in Egypt?"

Elbows told her.

-

"I was sitting in the basement bar of a hostel in Budapest, drinking Unicum with Ginger and two Brazilian

Jews named Andre and Roberto. Roberto's eyes looked both Middle Eastern and South American, misty as they peered out from beneath locks of dark, curly hair. Andre was the spitting image of Fidel Castro, right down to the chiseled beard and green army coat. So much so, in fact, that he was stopped at the Hungarian-Romanian border and asked, 'Are you a revolutionary?'

"Perhaps two dozen wind weary travelers warmed themselves at scattered tables and couches while we five talked diving. I told Andre and Roberto of America and Hawaii. They already knew of the Caribbean. Then, having just returned from a year on a kibbutz, Andre threw back a shot and spoke of the Red Sea."

Elbows wrinkled up his face, took on a thick accent, and pantomimed. "The Northern end of the Red Sea splits into the Gulf of Aqaba to the East and the Suez to the West. The break follows the Sinai Peninsula, across which Moses led our people and where he received the Commandments and thence to Jerusalem. Near the Southernmost point of land rests Sharm-el-Sheikh, a town of hotels and dive shops. A stone's throw from the beach the sea plunges to depth. It is filled with coral and Manta Rays and Jacks and sharks. Between Ras Mohammad, the southernmost tip of land, and the Suez Canal, rest dozens of World War II shipwrecks. The sea is deep and clear and glows red in the setting desert sun."

Elbows chuckled and returned to his normal voice. "The most pleasurable aspect of trekking through Europe is the countless stories told by wanderers from every fold of the globe. Ginger and I watched as Andre spoke of the Middle East in impeccable English, and then in Spanish, then Hebrew. He ordered more drink in Hungarian.

"A week later we headed for Vienna. Andre and Roberto remained in Eastern Europe before heading west and eventually home to Sao Paolo. We heard many more tales of travel, but none matched Andre's description of the Red Sea.

"Three months later and 1150 kilometers distant, we were walking down Harlemerstraat in Amsterdam when Ginger pointed to the window of a small travel agency. 'Isn't that the town Andre told us about?'

"In the window hung a whiteboard advertising 'last minute plane tickets' in Dutch and English. Beneath was a handwritten list of cities, prices, and departures – all in the next two days. Apparently the agency was hocking the empty seats on departing flights at bargain prices. London was there, and Frankfurt, Milan, Damascus, Cairo, and there at the bottom of the list, Sharm-el-Sheikh.

"'A C-note would bring enough guilden for two tickets,' she noted.

"'It's cold. Let's get something hot to drink.' We crossed the street to a bar and slipped inside.

"We had completed our clockwise circle of Europe and sat listlessly, contemplating stretching the road or flying home. I felt a changed person from the most extended travel of my life, but I was tired, and broke.

"'Why not Egypt?' It took her longer to ask than I thought.

"'Europe is one thing.'

"'What's the difference?'

'We could not hear it, but knew from the sudden drop in temperature that the door had just opened. Ginger's eyes widened as they lifted from mine and fixed behind me.

She was around me and hugging both Brazilians as Andre's resonant chuckle reached me. 'Mundo pequeno.'

"A Hindu would call it karma, a hippie would say it's fate. Hunter S. Thompson would say it was the Great Magnet.

"We had a round with Andre and Roberto, went across the street and bought our tickets. I had my gear shipped from the states. We were there for a year. When it was time to get back stateside I came here. Hamdullah.'"

"With Ginger?" Mercy asked.

"No."

"Who's Ginger?"

"Another time, Mercy." Elbows smiled. "How did you end up here?"

"I guess it's like you said, Elbows."

"How's that?"

"Another time." She grinned. "What does Hamdullah mean?"

It means, "thanks be to God," but it also means something like, "it is the Will of God."

"I don't get it."

"Say something good happens. You get a job, you get to go on a journey, you make a friend. You say 'Hamdullah' to give thanks. But say something bad happens, you lose a job, you have to say goodbye. It also applies. You say 'Hamdullah.' It is God's Will, and, the way I see it, we should still be thankful, whether you believe in God, or whether you think he speaks Arabic or English or Aramaic."

"He, huh?" Mercy raised her bottle and sipped her beer.

Recon

Kenny was different from most everyone else in the Marlin
in two distinct ways. First, he was stumbling *into* the bar,
and second, he had a plan. If he didn't know you by sight,
he had more money than you, though you could not tell
from the way he dressed. He had even removed the single
piece of opulence he allowed himself – an understated
Vacheron Constantin chronometer, and stuffed it into his
pocket a moment before entering. He plowed in sideways,
screwed his face into an angry sneer, and slapped his hand
on the bar's smooth, worn surface with an air of drunken
authority.

"Take it easy, mister," the bartender half-smiled,
half-growled. He did not make eye contact with the
drunken tourist. It both avoided potential conflict and
allowed him to watch a privileged young man hoist an
equally privileged young girl onto the pinball machine in the
corner. "What'll it be?"

"I want a shot of Cazadores, a Bud back, and Jack
Sweet's ass."

"No problem with the first two," replied the still-
preoccupied bartender as the drinks appeared. "What's the
issue with Sweet?"

"He's a good-for-nothing flake and a piss-poor
pilot."

"That's odd. Around here folks think he's top notch. In fact, you might be the first guy ever had the balls to say something about his character, and I *know* you're the first to criticize the way he flies. He's an ace. And I mean that literally."

Next to Kenny, a graceful woman shot him a chiseled stare from underneath a wave of auburn hair and over her shoulder as she took a younger man by the elbow and led him out the door. This was greeted with hoots and cheers from the rest of the gang, even the one facing the pinball machine.

Kenny watched her go and then turned his ire on the other patrons at the bar itself.

"I don't give a damn about tourist opinions, but if there's a local here who thinks Sweet's shit doesn't stink..." he paused to let the slur settle, "I wanna hear it." With that he tossed back the shot and smacked the glass down bitterly. He threw back his beer and treated it to a pummeling as well.

"Easy, partner," said the bartender, watching him carefully now that he thought this drunken tourist might actually be a problem. "This definitely ain't the place to walk around talking trash about Jack Sweet. He's one of the most well-liked guys in town."

"More popular than Lucky Tom?"

"You really don't know what you're talking about. Everybody thinks Lucky Tom is an asshole, even Tom himself. He's so goddamn cheap he won't eat. You seen how skinny he is? Christ, you think Lucky Tom is alright and Jack Sweet is a bum? You don't know shit."

"I know what's gonna happen when I find Jack Sweet." He gulped the rest of his beer.

The bartender shook his head. "Not if word gets around first, which it already has, and on top of that Jack Sweet could kick your ass when you're sober without breaking a sweat. You're in for a heap of trouble in this town, partner. Next boat leaves in half an hour, and if you like your skeleton the way it is, maybe you should see that it's on board."

At this a grizzled sailor across the bar who had been listening silently the whole time let out a soft chuckle. Kenny turned on him. "What's so goddamn funny?! You got a problem with me? Are you Sweet?"

"You know I'm not Sweet."

"I've never seen you before in my life."

"That's how you know I'm not Sweet."

"How do you figure that, old-timer?"

"Some folks around here aren't too hard to fool. Some folks. Don't get me wrong, I like your play. I'm anxious to see who you are and what kind of bird you're bringing over. And, I'll keep your little secret for now on one condition."

"What's that?"

"You let me watch you put on your act in the next bar."

"Deal."

No Mercy

"Come on, kid. It's just a little deeper. The same rules apply." Mercy cut the skiff's engine and allowed the craft to drift close enough to drop an anchor line. It was the young man's first deep dive, and she selected one of the most striking sites on the island - Ship Rock. The pinnacle rose out of the depths some 200 feet below, and a rich kelp forest embraced it with all the life it contained. Bright orange garibaldi peered out from behind the rocks, visible even from the surface. There was no bait in the water, but it still shone clear and cool beneath a cloudy sky.

"Remember, your air goes much faster at depth. Stay close, move slow, and watch your gauges," she cautioned.

"Yessir," he smiled in response. "I guess this is the weekend when you show me a whole new world."

"You're already a diver. This is just your first on a deep pinnacle."

"I wasn't talking about diving."

"Don't get cocky, kid."

The boy began to speak behind a wicked grin and Mercy silenced him with a stern look that turned into a bemused smile. She watched as he assembled his gear. He zipped his wetsuit closed over the blend of baby soft skin and granite hard muscle possessed only by males who are no longer boys but still working on becoming men. She helped him tuck into his rig. Watching a diver gear up is one of the best ways to gauge ability, and stress level, she thought to herself. This kid looked fine.

"Ready?" Mercy asked as she slid into her own gear.

"Affirmative."

Mercy rolled into the water first, and waited for him to join her. As they descended into the blue, Mercy's eyes grew wide. Sometime recently, an entire section of the pinnacle had sheared away and fallen into the abyss. The very face of the structure had changed, and though she had dived it dozens of times, if she hadn't dropped the anchor herself, she wouldn't have recognized it. What had once been an abrupt plunge into blackness was now a terraced fall, an insane giant's staircase.

The boy kicked ahead and beneath her, oblivious to the change - it was all new to him. The increasing water pressure began to squeeze his ears, and he reached up to pinch his nose and equalize the pressure. When he pulled his fingers from his nose, he caught a glint of metal on the steep slope. Above him, Mercy floated, weightless in the blue, astounded by the change and baffled by what might have caused it. The boy slipped deeper, fascinated by the gleam beneath him. His depth gauge crept past one hundred feet and still he dropped, drawn by the glow.

Mercy swiveled her head, surveying the new landscape. It was as if a giant chisel had pounded itself into the pinnacle at enormous intervals, punching away chunks of earth and flicking them into the abyss. The scars shone bare between the thick kelp forest on either side, scraped clean by a force she could not imagine. When she turned to look for the boy, he was gone.

No feeling of emptiness compares to that of a diver looking after another who looks back to discover their charge has disappeared. It can happen in an instant, and the feeling stays forever. Mercy was experienced enough not to panic. The first place to look is up, she thought to herself. Almost always, when a dive buddy goes missing, he has floated. Her stomach sank further when her upward gaze found nothing but water. Then she peered down, and caught the boy's bubble stream at the edge of her visibility. Air that had been in his lungs a moment before now rose in expanding spheres, flattened by the water resistance as they pushed upwards. Then the boy appeared beneath them and thrashed his way through his own bubbles, bolting for the surface. As Mercy kicked towards him she saw his eyes wide and glassed over with terror inside his mask. She was beside him in an instant, grabbing him, wrapping his legs with hers so he could no longer kick. She emptied the air from his buoyancy jacket, trying to slow him, but they still rose too quickly. Up through the water column they shot, outracing their own bubbles.

On the surface the skiff bobbed lazily in a light breeze, barely enough to ripple the water. A moment later the sea exploded as Mercy and the boy surfaced, almost breeching with their ascent speed. Mercy inflated the boy's jacket to keep him afloat, and gasped when she saw blood foam from his mouth with each ragged breath. She stripped off his weights and gear, and then hers, and in between mostly failed attempts at rescue breaths, managed to haul herself into the skiff and drag him in after her. She grabbed her handheld radio.

"Pongo, pongo, this is a twelve foot skiff at Ship Rock with an injured diver aboard. We need Baywatch." As she released the transmission button an invisible vice clamped down on her right elbow. The nitrogen in her blood, some from this dive, and more built up over the days before, screamed in protest at being brought to the surface so quickly. The gas exploded from solution and formed bubbles in her blood, foaming and frothing like a beer shaken and opened suddenly. They crowded and jammed into her joints and twisted her arm and then her back into the painful curve that earned it the nickname "the bends." She fell to the deck beside the unconscious boy as the radio crackled to life with a response from Baywatch. She lifted her head one final time to reach for the young man before her head thudded to the deck next to his.

The Agony of Sarmiento

When the *Desire* and *Content* navigated the Strait of Magellan in January, 1587, it was the height of summer, but still barren land slipped by on either side of the English cruisers, sometimes narrowing the channel to alarming proportions. They proceeded slowly and took frequent soundings, having no desire to run aground in this, the most inhospitable place yet discovered. As if to give evidence to this truth, they came across the ruins of Spanish settlements, and from the few survivors learned of the tragedy that befell the colony.

Following Drake's successful passage and subsequent attacks in the Pacific, a Spaniard named Sarmiento was sent to capture the English pirate when he tried to return home through Magellan's strait. Drake never did so, instead continuing up the coast perhaps as far as what would become Oregon, searching for the mythic Northwest Passage some thought would connect the Pacific to the Atlantic through the Great Lakes. Failing to find what was never there, Drake crossed the Pacific, explored the South Seas, and returned to England by rounding Africa and its Cape of Good Hope.

While waiting for Drake to return, Sarmiento exhaustively mapped the entire Strait of Magellan and the labyrinth of water ways and dead ends spreading like cracked glass from Cape Horn to him. Sarmiento became convinced that the Strait of Magellan was the key to the Pacific. When he realized Drake was not returning he sailed to Spain, begging King Philip to build a colony and forts there and secure the Pacific for Spain forever. Philip was none too pleased with Drake's surprise, and gave Sarmiento the Royal Blessing to proceed. The explorer mounted a fleet of 23 ships and 3500 men, and sailed back in September of 1581 to claim the entrance to their kingdom of gold.

A week from port in Spain, a gale struck and saw five ships and 800 men lost. The entire force returned home. Two months later they tried again. Somewhere in the Atlantic, the ship carrying the bulk of the colonist's stores went down with another 300 souls. When they finally reached port in Rio de Janeiro deserters numbered as many as faithful, and it was not until February of 1584 that Sarmiento returned to the strait to build his colony. He named it San Felipe. His sister ship abandoned him in heavy weather to return to Spain, carrying along with her much of the remaining sustenance of the colonists. Whether this was done willingly or out of necessity he could only conjecture. They now faced the harshest of southern winters before the first crops could be planted. They laid the foundations of two towns, determined to prevail. In April it began to snow, and it did so unceasingly for a fortnight.

Sarmiento realized that if they were to survive, he would have to go to a Spanish settlement for provisions. He sailed with that goal in mind, and was thrashed about so violently that he fled back to Brazil and the Atlantic to save his ship from sinking. The governors of the Spanish colonies unwilling to help him, he sailed back to Spain in defeat. The entire disaster earned the ire of Philip, and made Sarmiento perhaps the only Spaniard fortunate to be captured by the English. Sir Walter Raleigh seized Sarmiento and his ship as he attempted to return to Spain and beg forgiveness and help for his stranded colonists. Raleigh presented him to Queen Elizabeth, and it would be a long time indeed before he saw Spain again. With full knowledge of the potential of King Philip's temper, this was perhaps not entirely an accident.

Those who survived the first winter in San Felipe spent the following summer trying to gain a foothold for crops in the unforgiving soil and waiting expectantly for Sarmiento to return as their savior. When he never did, the fifty or so who still lived attempted to build two boats and flee their wretched destiny. One sunk almost immediately, and they abandoned their attempt and much of their hope. When Cavendish and Edmund arrived three years later, scarcely a dozen remained. One man, Hernandez, boarded the *Desire* and told his tale. As for the rest, despite their hideous condition they refused Cavendish's offer of passage to Peru, and chose to remain with some of their dead still lying in the streets of the town they must have felt was abandoned by their Captain, their King, and their God.

The Present

The doorbell rattled through the dim apartment, pinging off the glass of empty bottles and cardboard pizza boxes before finding its way into the bedroom. The second ring pulled Mercy's head from the pillow. She rose from the bed and rubbed her eyes, glancing down at the sleeping form next to her. He did not move, his head invisible under a pillow. She turned and made her way into the kitchen and then the living room, stepping gingerly over bottles and crusts, her sweats swishing against the faded carpet.

The blue shirt of a Flying Boats delivery boy appeared when Mercy opened the door.

"Package." He held a box as wide as himself, the signature pad pinched between it and his chin.

"I didn't order anything."

"You want to refuse it?"

"What is it?"

"Don't know. It's a bit heavy, if you get my meaning."

Mercy gave him a tired smile, pulled the pad from beneath his chin, and signed it. She tucked it back, pinched his cheek, and took the package from him. "It's not that heavy, junior." The delivery boy blushed, grabbed his signature pad, and spun away. Mercy backed into the apartment and closed the door with her knee, plopping down on the tired couch with the parcel on her lap. She froze when she saw the return address. "Holy shit."

Her keys lay on the coffee table, empty bottles of Coors standing sentinel. Mercy grabbed the key ring and used a key to part the packing tape. The box yawned open, and she fished an envelope from inside. The flap was folded under but not sealed, and she flipped it open with one hand. It drifted to the floor as she let it fall away from the letter inside, which she read aloud as the box began to shake atop her knees.

"I want this out of my house. It, and you, took my son from me. When he sailed to your god forsaken island he had my boat, my pride, my love. You took it all from me, took my son's future from me, and drowned it. I hear that you don't dive anymore, except into a bottle, and that's how it should be. My wife takes comfort in the fact that our boy is with God now, but people like you and me know what that's worth. The police investigation found nothing whatsoever wrong with his gear. Diver error. Well, here it is. Take it, throw it away, give it to somebody who knows how to use it safely. I want it, and you, out of my life forever."

Mercy resented the sting of tears at the corners of her eyes as she finished reading. She paused for a moment, and then let the letter fall to the floor as she stood with the package and marched to the door. Outside the morning sun began to slide towards midday, casting a short shadow behind her. In the alley the dumpster's lid was open, and Mercy flung the package inside.

Back in her kitchen, Mercy threw together a Bloody Mary and stared out the window. The light was not kind to the changes in her face since the last time she had seen that dive gear. The letter rested underneath her fingers, and nothing in the room moved save the slow rise and fall of her chest and the ice cubes as they settled into her perspiring drink. The sound of a trash truck approaching outside brought another tired smile to her face.

Mercy left the letter and the drink in the kitchen and disappeared outside. A puff of air lifted the letter and set a corner of it against the condensation on the glass as she opened and closed the door. The sound of male voices and a metallic rattle drifted in through the window, followed by the door slamming again. The package under one arm, Mercy reappeared and grabbed her drink and an ice bucket.

The couch groaned as Mercy settled into it. She shoved the package onto the coffee table, pushing empty bottles aside and onto the floor, making room for her to plop down the Bloody Mary. A muffled moan drifted out from the bedroom. "What the hell?"

"Sorry, Alex," she said with a sigh.

"Why don't you come back to bed?"

"Later."

"If you don't come back to bed, I'm going back to sleep."

Mercy ignored this and refocused on the package. She paused to breathe and then reached to touch it, gently, as if afraid to wake it. Finally she opened it. Pieces of dive gear began to emerge, hoses, gauges, a vest. The salt-dried fabric crinkled in Mercy's grasp.

"I should've never let you out of my sight." Her hands moved over the jacket, and paused over a concealed pocket. They probed inside and emerged with a chunk of dried coral the size and shape of a small cookie. Its edge gleamed gold.

"That wasn't there when we went in the water." She pulled at her drink and sniffled. "And you weren't there when we came out. Hell, there isn't even supposed to be hard coral in these waters." The coral rolled across her hand until the gleam caught her eye. She tabled the empty glass and peered at the coral. "What is this, one last surprise?"

Mercy pulled the ice pick from the bucket and began to chip away at the coral. A drift of dust accumulated on the table as the coral flaked away to reveal the rounded edge of a coin.

"Is this what got you all excited, kid?" She pushed the gear back into the package, rose from the couch, and pocketed the coin.

The Sacking of the *Santa Ana*

The galleon loomed closer, men visible on deck preparing defenses. They tossed protective netting over the holds and crouched behind cover, loading primitive muskets known as arquebuses. They had no canon. Cavendish saw some men readying piles of stone to heave onto their attackers. Cutlasses glinted in the sunlight. The *Desire* closed in while Edmund waited at his ordered distance, twisting the wood of the *Content's* helm in his hands until it groaned in protest. He was patient. The *Desire* continued to close and Edmund to tack, so that now the English and Spanish ships appeared of similar size to his woefully cool gaze. Cavendish's men stood ready, those in the boarding party clenching swords and hooks and still more loading canon and bracing the massive iron beasts in place. From this distance it was eerily silent, though Edmund knew there reigned a restrained exuberance punctuated with the sounds of effort and the panting of fear and expectation.

-

All spring of 1587 the ships had continued up the west coast of South America, visiting islands, bays, and native settlements. Sometimes the Indians approached in canoes bearing gifts of fresh meat and fruit. On other occasions, different groups decided to attack the landing party immediately. Edmund found it humorous that both gestures were for the same reason – the natives thought them to be Spanish. On the 18th of March, they missed their intended port of Valparaiso and ended up in the Bay of Quintero. Their presence alerted a Spanish alarm, and Edmund saw the lookout disappear over a hill and three Spaniards return on horseback. The *Desire* signaled him to stand off and not weigh anchor. He saw Cavendish launch a party of thirty in a long boat along with Hernandez as interpreter. The men returned to the *Desire* with the news that the initial exchange was profitable; the Spaniards had agreed to resupply the English.

The boat went a second time with Hernandez, and the second parley was not as successful. The English guard grew lax with the promise of cooperation, and Edmund watched through cupped hands as Hernandez leapt up behind one of the riders and the three galloped over the hill with Hernandez rescued from starvation by the English and restored to freedom by the Spanish. The English returned to the *Desire* and the crew of the *Content* heard the rattlings of Cavendish's wrath until sunset.

The next day, the nineteenth, a landing party filling water casks for the *Desire* looked up to see at least two hundred Spaniards gallop over the same hill that saved Hernandez. Twelve of the English found themselves cut off from the boats. Some fell to Spanish steel, some were captured, and men on the *Content* said two drowned when the *Desire's* boat fled without them. Edmund, again, watched the fight from afar.

Three times over the following months Edmund was allowed to help capture and sack Spanish ships. From one they hauled wine, from the other two nothing. Again, weeks later, they sailed into Arica and seized two ships.

They too lay empty. The Spaniards, alerted to their presence, had offloaded the ships' cargo. They stood ready to guard town from behind new defenses. Cavendish called off the attack and sent in a messenger. He offered to trade the captured vessels for his English comrades taken prisoner. Both sides waited for the Viceroy of Peru's eventual refusal. Cavendish and Edmund burned the ships to the bottom. Long after the flotilla departed, the captive English faced the Spanish Inquisition before hanging as pirates.

Thus they continued up the coast, seizing ships not alerted to their presence, sailing faster than the shouts of warning behind them, and landing and taking towns. Edmund marveled at the abundant shores, teeming with wildlife and fowl and cattle and horses. Again their masquerades were repeated with the natives, with submission and violence alternating. Again they surprised Spanish settlements and sacked and raided. When ambushed once more at Puna, Cavendish allowed Edmund to burn the entire town and the four ships under work there. Cavendish himself burned the Catholic church and ordered the bells seized. A prize, yes, thought Edmund, but treasure, no.

-

The *Desire* ran alongside the galleon. Edmund saw Cavendish at the helm, waving and shouting silently into the wind. He saw the boarders tense and then spring. Lines and hooks flew across and Cavendish butted the galleon with the stout side of his ship. Spaniards began heaving rocks down onto the attackers as they climbed and clambered. Edmund saw the flash and smoke of arquebuses and men fall before he heard the hollow boom.

The English replied with a musket volley of their own. Cries began to reach him across the water and he twisted the wooden helm, patiently.

The Spanish resistance grew in intensity and the boarders were killed or repelled. Edmund watched incredulously as some jumped into the ocean to escape the Spanish wrath. Cavendish did not stop to rescue them. Edmund sent his long boat to pull the men from the sea, and did not correct them when they appeared on board the *Content*, cursing the Captain who left them to drown.

The *Desire* attacked again, and the thin veneer of Cavendish's patience showed when the cannons roared and raked the deck of the galleon. A mast exploded in a shower of splinters and holes appeared in the tired ship's sides. Edmund now bore witness to the cunning of the admiral. Cavendish ordered the cannons reloaded and tilted down, pointing at the waterline of the Spanish prize. Simultaneously another boarding party attacked under cover of musket fire. One man lunged for the main mast and began climbing. Edmund wondered if it was personal valor or fear of disobeying Cavendish that sent him scurrying up the mast of the Spanish galleon. He succeeded in cutting free the main sail and held it in his hand as he plunged to the deck, arquebus balls punching through the fallen sail to kill them both. As the sail settled in a shroud over the sailor, Cavendish unleashed another cannon volley, tearing the Spaniard at her waterline. The ship coughed and writhed under her fallen sail as the sea poured into her fresh wounds and she began to founder. The Spanish captain raised the flag of truce.

Edmund cut slow circles around the two vessels, the *Desire* holding the galleon as a hunter grasps bagged game.

He watched a launch leave the galleon and swing around to convey messengers to Cavendish. Still he held his helm. None of his crew approached. Later the Spanish messengers emerged from the *Desire* and returned to their ship. Finally, Cavendish signaled him. They were towing the galleon to shore. He means to beach her before she sinks, thought Edmund.

As they neared land, dusk fell and Cavendish dispatched troops to patrol the galleon and see the pumps manned during the night. The Spanish appeared model prisoners to Edmund. They have already relinquished their treasure and now merely hope to escape with their lives, he thought. Cavendish had undoubtedly given such a promise. The men on the galleon's deck performed their duties and the pumpers stayed ahead of the leaks. It would remain to be seen whether the promise was kept.

With the dawn Cavendish ordered the galleon anchored in the shallows and the crew set ashore. Edmund anchored his ship and took a launch to inspect their prize. Some one hundred sixty souls began disembarking the galleon under guard. Many were crew, some Spanish passengers returning home from the Manila colony. Scores of slaves and servants splashed to the sand alongside their masters. Two young Japanese men emerged, blinking in disbelief, and huddled together on the beach, apart from the rest.

Then, finally, the treasure began to appear. Cavendish took the gold first. Chest upon chest was lifted to the deck and opened, each muscled about by two stout seamen, sweat dripping onto the riches of kings. Spanish coins known as cobs gleamed within, hundreds to a chest and scores of chests. Edmund tried to calculate the worth as Cavendish ordered the treasure rowed to the *Desire* and lowered into her holds. Edmund's men watched hundreds of thousands of coins pass between the ships. Their salary was roughly one of those coins a month, until today.

When the gold finally exhausted itself, the remaining treasure began to emerge. Pearls, silk, satin, damask, musk, spices, and all manner of strange jewelry tumbled from hand to hand to boat and finally piled on the beach. Edmund knew his men were already grumbling about the great wealth aboard the *Desire*. He would have to beg patience of them until they split the spoils. The Admiral merely wanted to secure the gold first. It was soon apparent that the galleon carried more than both English ships could hold, and there would be more than enough for all. He realized he was trying to convince himself, and shared his sailors' misgivings.

Finally, as the shades of evening drew forth, Cavendish announced the ship empty. Then he approached the passengers and even from the launch Edmund saw a heated discussion ensue. Fool, thought Edmund. As if speaking louder will make them understand English. He is trying to make sure no one is holding back. As if to prove his point, Cavendish sent a messenger to Edmund. Burn the ship.

-

Edmund kicked water from his boots and turned in the damp surf, watching the blaze grow. He liked the warmth on his face and the fear of the Spaniards and slaves on his back. He could not believe in what squalor the Spaniards held their captives. Malnourished and whipped, they did not appear overly displeased with the lot of their masters, though they clearly feared for their own. The

Japanese boys, however, were pacing about excitedly, lines of worry on their faces. They spoke to each other in a rapid, unintelligible tongue, and approached Edmund, pointing to him and to their smoldering ship. When a mast collapsed one cried out.

"Yes, I'm burning your ship," Edmund said. The two drew up close and for a moment he thought they would actually attack him. Then they passed and began making their way through the waves towards their burning boat.

"Hold!" Edmund shouted, pulling a short musket from his belt. The Japanese turned and looked at him. Over their shoulders Edmund saw a figure appear on the deck of the blazing ship. It moved about, shying from the flames, looking to shore and back. The boys began shouting towards it. The ropes from the rear deck blazed and began to give way, falling to the main deck with a hiss of sparks. The figure on board the galleon hesitated once more, and another falling rope tried to tangle in its hair. Then it plunged overboard and the boys, ignoring Edmund's shouts, ran out to meet it. As they grasped the figure under the arms and began to fight back to shore, it emerged from the orange glow a woman. Her features matched those of the boys, as did her look of terror, though it softened on her face, tempered by resignation, if not defeat. They broke from the surf and she collapsed on the sand, pausing but a moment and a single breath before looking up at him. Edmund felt the commotion behind him and anticipated Cavendish's noisy arrival. He saw in the boys' eyes relief in her survival, fear in her discovery, and defiance in her protection. They called her name, "Ina hime." Princess Ina.

All Edmund heard was "Ina." And he saw, beyond all he had seen that glorious day, an object of true treasure, an object for which he had been patient, and now, finally, an object worthy of being his.

The Coin

Dusty shutters covered the windows of the Marlin Club and kept the afternoon light at bay as Mercy tucked into a corner booth, talking to Elbows. He pawed a cocktail, occasionally sucking at it between grayish white whiskers. A bored waitress plunked down a beer and Mercy nursed it.

"I know he loves me, Elbows. He just doesn't like when I talk about, you know, the whole thing. He doesn't understand why I don't want to dive, why neither of us want to get married, why I don't want to, well, hell, when was the last time you met a guy younger than forty who could articulate a feeling at all?

"True to a point. You know the problem with adolescence in men?"

"Hmm?"

"It lasts the rest of our lives." Mercy chuckled and pulled at her beer. "Still," the old man continued, "I don't like the way he treats you, and not to be hypocritical, I don't much like the way you've been treating yourself of late." Elbows punctuated this by finishing his drink. "I know, none of my business."

"I think it's sweet that you think it is. Enough. Take a look at this."

Mercy slid the coral encrusted coin from her pocket, kept it below the table, and passed it to Elbows.

"This is not fresh from the mint. But it's not fresh out of the water, either. What's the story?"

"The boy found it."

"Let me guess when. How did it surface now?"

"I got a care package from his Dad this morning. It was in his BC pocket."

Elbows gestured to her beer. "I thought you were starting a bit early this morning, even for you."

"You're not drinking club soda, buddy."

"Merely expressing solidarity, my dear. Why did he send it to you?"

"To make sure I remember who to blame." Mercy exhaled over her longneck, which responded with a soft moan.

"It's not your fault and it's ancient history. Tell me about this. Hard coral doesn't grow here. Do what you were going to do - tell me about this."

"When I finally found his bubble stream, he was already bolting for the surface. He was terrified. Maybe he was excited when he found the coin. I don't know how deep he went, or what made him bolt. I should've grabbed him sooner."

"You did everything you could, and got bent in the process. You haven't been in the water since, remember?"

"The doctors cleared me to dive a year ago." Mercy motioned for another round. "It's like I don't deserve it anymore."

Elbows gestured to the coin under the table. "Then consider this a sign from the sea gods, or at least an asshole. Where was it?"

"In the small pocket hidden on the edge of the new Scubapro Classic buoyancy compensators. The one no one knows is there until you point it out."

"So he found this, stuffed it in his pocket, went for you, way too fast, panicked,"

"Let's skip the rest."

"And it sat in that pocket for a year while the investigators tested his gear."

"It was so selfish. I secretly hoped they would find a mechanical failure, a reason for what happened, a fault somewhere that wasn't mine."

"Mercy, it wasn't."

"Stop it."

"Alright, alright. So there it sat throughout the inquest. Then the family got the gear back, didn't want to keep it around, and sent it to you."

"He said he didn't want to see it, or me, ever again."

"I think we should honor his wishes."

Mercy glanced at her phone when it beeped. "Looks like the boss wants to go lobster diving before dawn. Guess who's driving the boat."

"He still gives you work, out of the water. He'd love it if you got back in."

"Yeah, Tom's all heart." She gave the old man an affectionate punch and made her way from the bar.

Elbows peered down at the edge of coin peeking up at him from beneath the table, wondering where it came from and who brought it to his part of the world.

One Adventure Left

The sky and the water were the same sooty black in the dark that is predawn. The skiff cut through the glassy ink made possible by the absence of wind and the outboard hummed smoothly. Two men sat forward, backs against the gunwales, legs crossed on the deck. One, Lucky Tom, owned the skiff, the dive shop, and a decent chunk of the island. Mercy perched astern, the throttle handle of the outboard that also served as rudder control tucked underneath her arm despite the calm weather. She thought her boss as stingy as he was skinny. He wouldn't pay to feed his own body. She knew he liked his nickname almost as much as his idea that he forced his own luck. He was tan and bald. He drew a disposable razor across his head and down his neck as the skiff motored down the coast. Mercy didn't know the other man, a large, soft, silent sort... so far. Her left hand grasped the bench beneath and her head turned from side to side, eyes cutting the dark for any sign of debris in the water. The men wore wetsuits and had their hands and their eyes on their dive gear. Both had been mumbling tunelessly and now they began to speak to one another. Mercy could hear them more clearly than they could hear each other as the wind caused by their forward motion pushed their words to her.

"What were you doing?" Tom asked the big man.

"When?'

"Just now."

"Same as you. Getting ready to dive."

"You were mumbling."

"No I wasn't."

"Yes, you were." Tom was right, but they had both been mumbling, thought Mercy. A small wave caught the bow and pitched it a bit. Salty mist spit into the boat but the men did not mind in their neoprene suits.

"I was praying," the big man said.

"Praying."

"Yes."

"What in the hell are you scared for? You told me that you've done hundreds of lobster dives."

"I have. You don't have to be scared to pray."

"So do you really believe all that, or is it just the routine you go through before you jump? You know, the way a batter will tighten his gloves and take a cut and dig in the same way every time, like the pitcher cares. It's either going low and away or straight at his friggin skull no matter what he does with his goddamn gloves."

"You want an answer?" Mercy did but she was not invited to speak. It was her job to drive the boat, wait for them to roll in, pull the skiff away to deeper water while the men scoured the bottom, stuffing early season lobster into the big mesh and canvas bags, and hoist first the bags and then the gear and then the men back into the skiff and take them home.

"I really believe. And I pray every day, and I believe every day." When Tom did not respond the big man defended himself. "There is a comfort and a certainty in that." He looked away to his left and opened a hatch near the bow and peered inside for a moment. "Whew," he whistled and closed the hatch.

"A certainty?" Tom sneered. "What the hell are you talking about? How can you be certain that something you, hell no one, has ever seen or proven or documented or... anything for crissakes, exists?"

They stopped talking for a moment and readied their gear for the dive. Both were meticulous and each followed a pattern, Mercy noticed. Lucky Tom began to mumble again. Mercy wasn't sure but guessed it was part of his routine for gearing up. She had worked for Tom for two years now but had never heard this.

"Religion has caused way more damn trouble than it's fixed. Most every war was and is either for or against or mostly because of a dumb ass religion."

He clamped the webbing and buckle of his tank harness closed with a clank, popped the rubber dust cap from the tank valve, dropped the first stage of his regulator onto it and spun the yoke screw down snug to hold it in place. He opened the tank valve and heard it hiss and sigh as his system pressurized. He was pissed at his companion. Pissed he had let his crew talk him into taking the guy not only diving, for crissakes, but lobster diving. The first week of the season, during his secret time of day, and to one of his secret, golden spots. He noticed that in his contempt he had forgotten to hook up the hose that would inflate his buoyancy compensator to make him weightless under water. It was no big deal, and he simply forced it onto his inflator against the air pressure in the hose, hearing it hiss and snap as it locked into place. He hit his inflator button to test it and the air cell on his harness puffed out a bit to confirm all was in order.

"It was okay for us to come to this continent, absolutely murder, rape, and pillage anything we damn well felt like because the natives weren't the same religion we were and therefore were not people and we therefore had an excuse signed by your god himself. Columbus refused to convert the 'Indians' to Christianity because then, by law, he couldn't enslave them. Forget not enslaving them, just don't make them Christians - yet. It was pretty much the same thing for centuries. No decent God-fearing Christian could chain and whip and destroy generations of families and entire cultures if their prey were other children of God, but they weren't and I guess it's okay to treat animals that way. The Holocaust? Religion. Those guys who flew those airplanes into those buildings? Those heinous murderers from evil countries like the Commander-in-Chief liked to call them? They didn't think they were evil. They were the most righteous of the flock and would go to their heavenly reward for doing the Work of Allah. Just like those good Christians in Salem who proved their faith by tying a five year old girl to a stake and lighting the bale of hay underneath her on fire. Fucking religion."

Mercy had never heard words like these before and they pushed into her chest and made it hard to breathe. True, thoughts of similar flavor danced in her mind, particularly the last year. A bit of wind kicked up as the dawn drew closer and Lucky Tom motioned for her to slow down. They were nearing the site. Tom lifted his dive light and threw its beam towards the shore, looking for the landmarks to guide him to his secret spot. He had more than one GPS device, and trusted them. But he did not trust that they gave such precise numbers and if the numbers existed they could be stolen and with them his secret and so he did not use a GPS for lobster diving and as long as he could trust Mercy there were no numbers to steal.

The men slipped into their gear. Tom was quicker, his streamlined web harness wrapped simply over his shoulders and around his waist, the tiny buoyancy air cell behind him. It tended to float him horizontally, which put his face in the water even when he was on the surface, but he didn't spend much time there anyway. Once a customer had joked that his BC would drown him face down one day and Tom replied that if it did he wanted to be buried in the same position so the world could kiss his ass.

The other, bigger and gentler man took a moment to slide his thick arms into his rig. His BC wrapped all the way around him like a down vest, and inflated like a life jacket. It was called a stabilizing jacket for this reason, but Tom hated the bulk and the restriction to his movement. He had rinsed his first and only stab jacket after diving it once and put it back on the rack of his shop and sold it to someone else.

"Faith is a great comfort. I'm not saying that people haven't done some horrible things in the name of religion, but that's not religion. That's man's failure to live up to what religion is supposed to be. I'm going to venture a guess that politically you're pretty conservative."

Tom smiled. "Most rich people are. Like Churchill said, if you're not liberal when you're young, you don't have a heart. If you're not conservative when you're old, you don't have a brain."

"Gun control?"

"Hell no."

"So it's the same. You don't blame the gun when it is used to kill someone. It could've been used for food, or for protection, or not at all. But it was the person who committed the crime, not the gun. Don't blame God because people committed, and commit crimes in His name. There were a lot of people who always thought slavery was wrong. There were a lot of Germans sickened by the Holocaust, and most Muslims don't think the terrorists are enjoying their celestial virgins right now."

"God is a gun?"

"God is everywhere and everything and was and is and will be forever and forever. It is what we do with his teachings that's important." The big man reached down for his empty lobster bag. He took a large carabiner clip and snapped it onto the thick steel handle of the bag, and then clipped it onto a hefty D-ring on his jacket and spun the locking screw into place. He squeezed the D-shaped clip in his fleshy hand to make sure it was secure and the lock screw left a red circular indentation in the center of his palm.

Tom drew a slow breath. "I will grant one thing. I consider myself a bit of a gambler as well, and I like to figure odds. In a way everything is odds. Walking across the street to see a friend, you're taking a one in a million chance you're going to get run over so that you can hang out, drink a beer, get laid, whatever, and again when you come back home. We're taking a chance on this dive, just like on every dive, but we do things to stack the odds, like safety checks and buddy team and surface support and then we take the chance and do the dive."

"Not all people see it that way."

"Doesn't matter whether you see it or admit it or acknowledge it or not, that's the way it is."

"Maybe that's the way it is with God."

"Einstein looked for God in the numbers. He said, 'God does not play dice with the Universe.' And he knows more than we do."

"Einstein or God?"

"Both."

Tom scanned the shoreline and nodded in approval. "Here's the spot. Neutral, Mercy." She twisted the throttle and the propeller beneath them slowed its slicing through the water and stopped and the skiff drifted with diminishing momentum.

"There's one more thing. Humility. Faith puts you in your place and reminds you that you're not in charge, that there's something bigger and more powerful out there to be respected."

"Like the ocean."

"Precisely."

"But I can touch and see and feel and respect the ocean. And a gun."

"Good. Maybe someday you can do that with God, too." The skiff drifted and the now persistent gentle breeze began to blow more earnestly.

"When I said I liked looking at the odds I was trying to agree with you."

"Really?"

"I know there's no scientific basis for the whole Intelligent Design thing, but I like the idea. I like playing the odds and when I look around at the beauty and symmetry in the ocean and sky and on paper and in trees and everywhere, I wonder. I really do."

"I think it's good you pretend to have an open mind."

"Asshole."

"God willing."

They both laughed and so did Mercy. Perhaps these testosterone junkies needed a little perspective. She said, "I'll tell you one thing. If you're right and there is a God, I still don't think there's a heaven and a hell. If there's a God, that's her big joke."

"Her?!"

"I think that if there is one, it's definitely a she. Look at the ocean, look at nature, mother, right? At least that's what you should tell the girls." The men laughed again.

"So what's the joke?" Tom pressed.

"If there's a God and if she created this for us, the joke is simple - this is heaven. There is no great beyond or fiery pit, this is it. Look at us, we have every natural resource and every physical and mental ability and all the imagination and energy necessary to make every man, woman, and child happy. We could have libraries and parties and events and competitions and science and art and beer and orgies and peace and instead we're fucking it up. War and pollution and crime and the evils of organized religion. I don't know if there's a God. I do know that if there is, she's pissed."

The men pulled on their fins and reached for their masks and gloves.

"So if we treated each other and the planet well that would prove God exists, or at least make it more likely?" Tom asked. Mercy said nothing.

"I guess I'm okay with that," said the big man. "Method is secondary to effect."

The men put on their gloves and raised themselves to the gunwales and spit into their masks and rubbed. Then they reached behind them from the now motionless boat and dipped their masks in the dark water. They rinsed and put them on and pulled their thick hoods up so they could no longer hear one another. Lucky Tom motioned for Mercy to kill the motor. He didn't trust the propellor or anyone that much. She knew she was not to start the engine until their lights were down and well away.

They wrapped their lips around their mouthpieces and breathed deeply, watching the needles on the pressure gauges. Their eyes roamed over one another's gear, double checking, and then with a nod they rolled over backwards simultaneously, away from one another and into the water.

Neither man surfaced, in a bit of a show of style, and they kicked slowly downward, diagonally towards shore and the bottom, as they switched on their lights. They were expensive torches and showed bright and far. Now they illuminated nothing ahead or beneath them but black water. It was cold and the water pressed in on their ears. The big man pinched his nose through his mask and equalized. Tom worked his jaw and his ears popped, the compressed air he breathed slipping up his eustachian tubes to settle against the backside of his eardrums and flatten them against the water pushing in.

Their depth increased and they kicked side by side, their lobster bags unrolling and flapping on their chests and bellies. Tom played his light down and still saw nothing but black. He equalized again and glanced at his depth gauge. They were at nearly 100 feet and still no sign of bottom.

They had rolled in too goddamn far from shore. He glanced over and saw the big man already looking at him, signaling to level off. Tom glanced at his air and saw he had used less than 400 of his 3000 psi, despite the depth. They swam towards shore, and Tom slowed his breathing still further to conserve air. He had just begun to worry that his heading was off and they were lost in the dark and would have to surface to gain their bearings and that would take air and cut their dive time in half. Then he saw bottom. He gestured to the big man's computer and he pivoted it, showing better air consumption than Tom's own. They neared the sloping sand and the dive was on.

Mercy sat motionless in the skiff as the men descended, watching the glow from their lights grow dimmer and merge into one and then wink out entirely. She thought of what they said and of the blackness of the ocean and the sky and remained so until the wind strengthened and shifted and she felt it on her face. Images of the accident at Ship Rock crawled from her belly and into view. She blinked them back, angry at the wind for making her eyes water. The bubbles from the men's breathing rose to the surface and bubbled gently beyond the bow of the skiff, then moved slowly away.

The wind pushed hard against her right cheek. She had never felt a breeze kick up so suddenly this early in the day. A small chop grew on the surface and rolled towards shore. The boat was moving that way now, too, and Mercy pulled to start the motor.

The engine would not catch and she tried again and again. She tried the choke and twisted the throttle a bit and squeezed the bulb on the fuel line to force fuel into the engine though she feared she would flood it.

"Goddamn it, can't a girl catch a break?" She pulled again and again and still nothing. In a moment she would be dangerously close to the rocks. Mercy hurried forward and opened a hatch. Inside sat the anchor. It was far too big for the boat and almost too much for her, but when Lucky Tom went big he went big.

Mercy grunted and hoisted the anchor from the hold and toppled it into the water.

In her haste she neglected to thread the heavy chain over the roller on the bow and it clattered over the fiberglass of the side. Small white chips flew and she knew Tom would be pissed. Then the chain was gone and it was the rope hissing, but only for a moment, for then it slowed as the anchor thudded into the shallow bottom. Mercy let a bit more line out and moved it onto the roller and then tied it off. The boat moved closer to shore and the line grew tight and immediately held. The stern of the skiff swung around as the bow pivoted on the taut line and then she was into the wind and secure and the boat was safe.

One hundred twenty feet below and at least twice as far upwind, and up current, Lucky Tom and the big man kicked along the edge of a deep reef. To their right the bottom sloped away to sand, and on their left a tumble of rocks served as anchors to the massive lengths of bull kelp enveloping them. The kelp leaves grew a foot or more wide and some were thirty feet long. They covered the reef in a ribboned curtain and had existed for millennia as the basis for life on these same rocks. They showed their deep greens best when illuminated by white light, and the men's torches startled small fish and reflected pinpoints of light from mysterious eyes peering from under the rocks and kelp.

The lobster appeared suddenly. Several of them scuttled from the glare as they emerged from the dark. They had been scavenging the sand all night, and were now returning to the safety of the reef as dawn approached. Lucky Tom planned it so he was between them and the shelter of the rocks and kelp and it was his favorite time of day.

As Tom neared the closest and one of the largest of the lobster, he moved his light away so only the outer halo illuminated the bug. It's primitive brain calmed, and Tom distracted it with the beam of light just to the edge of its vision while he descended quietly from above. As he neared he held his breath so as not to be betrayed by bubbles. He knew beginners were taught to never hold their breath while diving. Doing so and ascending could literally rupture lungs as the compressed air inside expanded with the diminishing water pressure. Still, there was no harm in doing it while descending, free divers did that every day, on scuba you just had to remember to start breathing again on the way up. Tom held his breath and dropped quietly until the lobster was within reach.

Tom shot his thick-gloved hand downward and pinned the lobster to the sandy bottom. It was a big bug and he could barely afford a grip. It gave a tremendous buck and tried to shoot backward, flexing the massive muscle that was its tail and the object of human desire. Tom almost lost his grip and pushed down again, dropping his light and grabbing the base of the antennae with his other hand. The light settled butt down as it was designed to do, and shone on the reef sloping up. He knew that Pacific lobster have no claws to concern divers, but are much faster than their Atlantic counterparts. He stabilized his grip and lifted the lobster and it thrashed its tail again. The strength was unbelievable but he had it now and brought it to his chest and thrust it into the mesh and canvas bag using the one-way slit built for this. He released the carapace inside his bag and drew his hands out quick and flat and made sure the slit closed. The bug thrashed about in the mesh, knocking into his belly and his leg and then quieting.

He was in a cloud of silt now and moved towards the glow of his light. When he found it he pushed off the bottom to get above the silt and get his bearings but the weight of the lobster brought him back down. He inflated the air cell on his harness a bit, and this time floated up easily from the bottom, inhaling to gain momentum and blowing out to neutralize his buoyancy and level off.

Tom saw the glow of the big man's light ahead and swam. When he was close enough he shone his light on the sand in front of the big man and moved the yellowish circle in and out of the other beam, getting his attention. The big man turned in the water and smiled. Tom could see that his bag was full. Bastard. He smiled. But he had the biggest one and he'd get some more on the way back.

An air check showed they were both below half a tank and they immediately turned and began to make their way back and into shallower water. With each few feet of gradual ascent along the slope the air expanded and squeaked from their ears into their throats for them to breathe out. They were careful to move up slowly and gradually as they swam along the bottom, to keep the extra nitrogen their blood had absorbed from forming bubbles as they put the tremendous weight of the water beneath them.

They were over the rocky reef and kelp and then another stretch of sand. No lobsters showed on this one. Twilight was ending and Tom was down to 1000 psi when they saw the anchor. It snaked in and out of three boulders nestled at the edge of the sand, tougher cousins of the thousands of smaller rocks that spilled the length of the reef.

Tom wanted to know who the hell had followed them to his secret spot and what the hell they were doing so close to shore and how Mercy was handling all this. She was out to sea a couple of hundred yards with the engine running, waiting for them to surface so she could putter in and pick them up. He took another look at the anchor and wondered, or is she? The big man was examining the anchor and the boulders when Tom signaled him again with his light. Tom pointed to his air gauge and the big man looked at his own and signaled OK. Tom gave him the thumbs up and began to ascend along the anchor line. They were less than 30 feet deep and Tom wanted to know what was up. The big man pointed to himself and then to the bottom to indicate he was staying put.

Tom broke the surface 30 seconds later and wasn't much surprised to see Mercy looking at him over the side of the boat. He thought he'd recognized his bad-ass anchor.

"What the hell are you doing?"

"The engine wouldn't start and the wind was pushing me towards the rocks so I threw out the anchor."

"What did you do to the engine?"

"I don't know. It wouldn't start so I tried the choke and then I tried the throttle and the bulb and then I was out of time so I threw the hook in."

"Lucky you didn't bean us. You flooded the engine."

"Yeah."

"Cut the throttle all the way back and pull the choke and try it again. And make sure it's in neutral." He heard a shuffling and then Mercy's efforts pulling and the engine caught.

"Good." Now, I'm going down to get the hell out of the way of the prop and grab a couple more tails. Pull the anchor and get away from shore and when we surface come and get us like we planned."

"Got it."

Tom popped his regulator back in, looked to see his needle in the yellow between 1000 psi and the red danger zone of 500 psi as he moved down the anchor line. He had neglected a safety stop his last time up and another couple minutes on the bottom would be just fine as well as get him away from the spinning propellor. He felt Mercy above him, pulling on the line and, in effect, pulling the boat towards the anchor. Then he was back on the bottom and it was getting bright enough to see without lights. No more lobster this dive.

The anchor sat in twenty eight feet of water, jammed against one of the boulders and mocking him with the layers of chain twisted about the rocks. The big man caught his eye and gestured up and then to each of them. Tom nodded. Yeah, that's our boat.

Mercy had managed to pull the line and chain tight and they both saw that the anchor would have to be freed by hand. Tom checked his gauge and decided they could try for a minute or two at most and then, screw it, they would cut the anchor and come get it later. If he was forced to return, Tom determined he would bring a lift bag. The heavy airtight bag could be unrolled underwater and attached to the anchor with lengths of rope. Then the bag would be inflated with air from the tank. As it filled and rose to the surface, it would lift the anchor for him. Should keep a couple of lift bags on board, he thought.

When he looked back the big man was under a length of chain and his lobster bag was trapped between the anchor and the boulder. The big man struggled to free it, and the swinging chain buffeted his tank and the back of his head.

Lucky Tom rushed over and pushed everything, the man, the chain, and the bag to the side of the boulder. The big man inflated his safety jacket, trying to get free, and it buoyed him up in the water. His lobster bag remained pinned tight between the edge of the anchor and the rock. Then the big man ran out of air.

Tom saw his eyes go wide and he tugged once more on the anchor but the weight of the boat, the efforts of Mercy, and the elements were against him. Tom jerked his backup regulator from its holder and held it towards the big man. The big man grabbed it from him, spit out his own useless reg and jammed Tom's in his mouth. He coughed and choked and pressed the purge button, forcing air through the reg and sending a cloud of bubbles up and then he was breathing.

Now here we sit, thought Tom. That's what they teach you. Stop. Breathe. Think. Act. He checked his air. 400 psi and two frightened men breathing from one tank. He saw the big man fumbling with the heavy carabiner, trying to unscrew the lock and push it open and free himself from the bag. His buoyant vest floated him and held the tangle tight and they could find no purchase on the carabiner or on the bag. Tom fumbled for the valve to vent air from the big man's jacket and couldn't find it. Tom tried to tear the handle from the bag, then tried his knife, but the metal handle wound round the entire perimeter of the bag, for strength.

Tom's thoughts rattled in his brain as he checked his air gauge again. 200 psi. Way into the red. Pull the reg from the big man's mouth and ascend. No. He believes in God, he'll be in heaven. And you're going to hell. I don't believe in hell, but if I leave him here I'll already be there. So save him. For selfish reasons. Tom braced himself against the top of the boulder, the octopus hose now snaking dangerously down and around to the reg the big man held frantically in his mouth. Tom pulled with all his might and the bag held fast. He felt it growing more difficult to breathe as the last of the air bled from his tank.

Please God, oh please don't let this poor son of a bitch die or me either.

He pulled again and the boat suddenly moved above and the bag rolled under the edge of the anchor and they were spinning and then being dragged through the sand.

In the boat Mercy knew the anchor was tangled and could tell by the bubbles that the men were working to free it. She could've played out slack to help them but was afraid to because she was so close to the rocky shore. Finally the strengthening wind helped her decide which rule to break. She could tell the divers were on the bottom and it would be safe to gun the engine enough to put slack in the line and move away from shore. Then they would free the anchor and she could swing to sea and they could clean up their mess. I wonder if there are lift bags on board, she thought. She checked the lights again and noticed the bubbles coming harder now, a small spot in the ocean boiled. Fear grew in her belly and she again blinked back memories. Mercy gunned the boat away from shore, pulling the anchor and the chain and the line with it as it surged for deeper water.

The big man felt the last of the air go and dimly remembered the horrible tug of the bag going. Then the air was gone and Tom was gone and so was the anchor and so was which way was up. He floated in the darkness, utterly alone, and there was nothing else and with his last thought before everything went black he wondered if he would have to wait longer or if this nothingness was the biggest disappointment of all.

Tom shot for the surface, exhaling as he went, fearing for his lungs, fearing for everything. He looked up and saw the surface close and he knew he was going too damn fast and he didn't care until he heard the propellor.

The big man drifted alone, his arms stretched out, and his safety jacket expanded and raced for the surface with him in it. Faster they went and on the boat came, propellor churning, Mercy at the controls, trying desperately to get out of the way of whatever was happening below and stay off the rocks. The wind didn't care and the water didn't care and the rocks either didn't care or were amused. The big man struck the keel of the boat so hard he bounced back down and to the side as the propellor raced past, slicing into the remnants of his bag and cleaving the only lobster left inside neatly in half. The pieces drifted back down to the reef to be consumed and recycled as the big man broke the surface and his jacket rolled him upright.

Sound travels so fast underwater that even minute vibrations are distinct and engines are roars. Unfortunately, this same speed also makes it impossible to tell from which direction the sound is coming. The ears and brain can't triangulate. Things happen too fast. Tom remembered this bit of trivia as the engine grew in his ears and then he heard the tremendous thunk of something hitting the hull. He was out of air anyway so fuck it and he blasted through the surface of the water ten feet from the skiff just as Mercy cut the engine.

Mercy stopped the boat and reached over the far side. Tom was yelling and then he heard Mercy yelling. "Help me, Tom. I can't get him in the boat by myself. Tom! Goddamn it!"

Tom kicked to the boat, laying on his back and hollering some more. He made the far side of the skiff and saw Mercy holding the big man, whose head lolled senselessly against the edge of his jacket. Tom swam over and pushed as best his trembling body could while Mercy pulled. Finally the big man tumbled into the skiff, moaning softly.

Tom wondered if they were being blown towards the rocks. They were not. He noticed there was no wind and the sun began to rise. He looked at Mercy and Mercy looked at the big man as his eyes fluttered open.

"Jesus Christ. You okay?" Tom panted.

"I think so. We'll know for sure soon." The big man flexed his fingers and wiggled his toes, feeling for the bastard nitrogen bubbles that cause the bends. The sea was dead calm.

"I don't think I'm bent," Tom said. "I'm lucky I didn't burst my goddamn lungs. Good thing we were shallow."

"What the hell happened?" The fear and irritation in Mercy's voice were obvious. She didn't even dive anymore, and was still putting up with this shit.

"Just take us home," her boss ordered. She did.

The full glow of a clear dawn shone down on the dock as Mercy tied the skiff and began offloading gear.

"You sure you're okay?" the big man asked Tom.

"I'm fine. Born lucky. You?"

"Just a goose egg. Yeah, thank God."

"Yeah?" Tom looked at the big man and then at the ground and finally at the sea. "Maybe. Maybe not. Either way, we've all got at least one adventure left."

"Yeah." The big man grabbed his gear, gave a perfunctory wave, and walked away.

The big man would return to his world and tell everyone how his life had been saved. Lucky Tom would earn another notch in his nickname and celebrate the roll of the dice that had again gone his way. They would never see each other again and never tell anyone what they had really thought that night. Tom turned to Mercy.

"What are you looking at?"

"There's no right answer to that question, is there, Tom?"

"I think you're bad luck."

"I think you're right."

"I think you're fired."

"Now I know I'm right." She grabbed her bag from the skiff and followed the big man's path down the dock. Halfway to land, she turned.

"Oh, Tom?"

"What?!"

"You're welcome."

Elbow's Place

Nautical paraphernalia worthy of a museum populated Elbow's cluttered digs. Ship's wheels, anchors, compasses, and photographs of vessels at sea, in museums, and on the bottom adorned the walls. In contrast, one alcove appeared to be reserved for artifacts from the Far East. Delicate vases, paintings on rice paper, a Daisho set of long and short swords paired in a wooden holder met Mercy's eyes. Underneath rested the matching Tanto knife. Behind the swords sat a helmet that curved to protect the back of the head and neck. A cumbersome, yet foreboding crescent moon of steel perched atop it.

"Without the crescent, it reminds me of Darth Vader's helmet," Mercy said.

"Lucas got a lot of his inspiration from the East. I wouldn't be surprised. This is a replica of the helmet worn by the Date clan. Scared the shit out of their enemies. Their leader, Masamune, wore it later in his career. He was a fearsome samurai, and founded the city of Sendai."

"That's been in the news lately."

"It sure has."

Mercy and Elbows made their way past the remarkable clutter and into the kitchen. He opened the fridge and retrieved two beers.

"This is not an endorsement."

Mercy smiled. "Then we'll call it lubricating fluid for our research."

They passed through the kitchen and into a small makeshift lab. A few pieces of chemistry equipment occupied tables, while anchors, chunks of coral, old chain, and other indistinguishable oddities crowded around for a look. Elbows picked up a plastic container half filled with a pale solution.

"This should have enough punch to clean your find without damaging it."

He dropped the chunk of coral into the weak acid bath, donned thick rubber gloves, and began working it as the solution hissed softly. Mercy sipped her beer and watched.

"So after all that the son of a bitch fired you for good."

"I told you he was all heart."

"Speaking of big hearted men, where's your boy Alex?"

"He was so angry I lost my job he just left. He's improving. A year ago he would've punched something first."

"You?"

"I may not be on top of my game, Elbows, but I'm no pushover. A guy hits me, he loses at the very least the guilty appendage. That's if he's lucky."

"So inanimate objects bear the fury?"

"Bore it. I told you, he's working on his temper. And getting better."

"You certainly have a lot of faith."

"I don't think that's true. I don't think I have much any of that."

"And who's fault is that?"

"Who says that's a fault?"

Elbows continued to work and then lifted the cleaned coin from the solution. It glowed faintly.

"It's a cob. This was cut off the end of a bar or rod of gold, and then stamped, all by hand." he looked closer. "Yup. Spanish. That means it came across the Pacific on the Manila Galleons. But there's no reason for it to be this far North. When the Spanish sailed East with their spoils, they headed for what is now Acapulco. The riches were loaded onto mules, hauled across the peninsula, reloaded on ships, carried through the Caribbean and across the Atlantic to home."

He rinsed the coin and handed it to Mercy. She plunked her beer on the lab table and turned the coin over in her hands with the same sad, gentle grace that she had touched the parcel.

"So old..."

Elbows smiled at her and shook his head. His scraggly grey beard swished in agreement. "This coin this far north matches my crazy old theory."

"What's that?"

"The coin is Spanish, but maybe the wreck it came from isn't."

"Pirates?"

"English. If you were Spanish, they were pirates. If you were English, they were heroes."

"Didn't you mention something once about the power of perspective?"

"The winners write the history books."

"Tell me about it."

"After Magellan discovered the straits in 1520, the Spanish considered the Pacific to be their private back yard, and they wasted no time in exploiting it and reaping treasures from the East - gold, silver, silk, spices. At the time some of the spices were worth as much as gold.

Francis Drake managed to get a small fleet of English vessels into the South Pacific in 1579, and they went to town on the Spanish. Many of the galleons didn't even have cannons in those days. But Drake managed to circumnavigate and return home safely. No, this isn't from Drake. Next came Cavendish."

Mercy stole a glance at him. "I've read about them. But Cavendish made it home safe, too. He followed Drake's route."

"He did, but one of his ships didn't. Cavendish was captain of the ship *Desire*. But he had a second ship - the *Content* - which disappeared in 1587 after they sacked one of the most famous galleons of all time - the *Santa Ana*. The Spanish weren't expecting any resistance. They saw Drake as a lucky fluke, a miracle that he even made it into the new ocean. They weren't ready for a fight. They left most of their cannons in the Philippines to make room for more treasure."

"Cocky."

"You remember what I said about men? The English forced the *Santa Ana* aground. According to the only histories we have, that's where things went south. Cavendish loaded all of the loot on the *Desire*. Nothing went on the *Content*."

"That must've gotten some sailors sideways."

"Precisely my thoughts. And the next day, after the English burned the *Santa Ana* to the waterline and departed, the *Content* was lost in fog and never seen again. They never reunited. The *Desire* circumnavigated and returned home with, literally, a king's ransom. The *Content* was lost to history."

6th November 1587

Ina looked up at Edmund standing over her, and recognized the look on his face. She had seen it in the faces of the men who killed her father and burned her home and she knew what they did to her mother. She had not cried, not in front of them, and not now.

The Spanish Captain had protected her from his men. At first she was angry, and would have gladly died with her family. Once on board the galleon she became grateful for his protection, and while weeping silently in her dank hold, she regained the desire to live, knowing her parents would want her to fight, and when necessary to die with dignity. Later she came to resent the Spaniard as much as his men, learning from the Japanese brothers captured along with her that she was intended as a gift for the King. The Captain was protecting her only to increase her value and his eventual reward. He was just as selfish and evil as the man standing over her now, the only difference was patience.

Edmund reached down and yanked her to her feet, his hand wrapping completely around her arm. He had not felt the flesh of a woman since Guatulco, and he had never felt flesh like this. He sighed as he stared into her eyes, surprised when she returned his gaze.

"Why did you hide? You deserve to burn."

She said nothing, her face betrayed nothing. No fear, no surprise, no anger. Nothing. Edmund closed his right fist, and with deliberate caution struck her in the face just hard enough to split her lip without damaging her perfect teeth. She inhaled sharply, but her gaze did not change. Edmund drew back his fist again, and the brothers lunged between them, one driving Edmund backward while the other wrapped his arms around the young woman.

Suddenly the Navigator was beside him, an arquebus leveled at the defiant boys. Edmund found his own pistol in his hand a moment before he found his senses.

"Wait."

"We kill the men right now sir, then she's all ours," the Navigator growled.

"You fire that gun and Cavendish's men will be here in seconds. He'll take the girl, and you'll end up with an empty gun and one extremely upset Captain with a loaded one."

"Yessir."

"Call our guard, shackle them, take them below, and tell no one."

"Yessir."

As the guards chained the young woman to the men and led them across the sand towards the *Content*, Edmund noticed her staring back over her shoulder at him, that same placid look on her face. It made him smile and his teeth glowed in the flames of the smoldering galleon.

Recon Alex

Alex's head wasn't the first to turn when the blonde swung into the bar. Cool weather wool covered everything except her face, and succeeded in concealing nothing. That, thought Alex, is success. She walked up to him like she was looking for him. At this the locals turned and dutifully pretended to ignore them, straining necks and ears in a pitiable display.

"Hello Alex," the words came out buttery and thick with a Spanish accent that stood in such contrast to her fair hair and skin that it surprised him as much as her approach. Her mittens disappeared into pockets but she ordered nothing. "What, is it that I know your name, or that I don't look and sound the same color?"

"I don't know your name." Alex pushed a length of straight brown hair from his blue eyes, across an unremarkable nose, and looked again.

"Good. Then we can talk. I heard your girlfriend lost her job."

"You seem to know a lot about me. I suppose if you really did, you'd know that she lost her job a couple of years ago. Tom just kept her around doing dry work. Filling tanks, driving the skiff, that sort of thing. I don't think he gives a damn about her, he just likes the eye candy."

"She does have a glow, despite her age. She hasn't dived since the accident?"

"Who the hell are you?"

"I am no one. I am a voice, a messenger. You could look me in the eyes, you know." Alex said nothing and shifted his gaze to the door. "What matters to you is that I represent someone who has been watching you for some time. Someone with a proposition for you and your girlfriend. A very generous proposition, even before she lost her job."

"If you're so interested in Mercy, why don't you talk to her?"

"Because you're more approachable. And more sensible." She smiled and encouraged his eyes to wander back.

"What should I call you?"

"Señora. Let's go."

"If I walk out of here with you, people will talk."

"They're talking already. Come on, he wants to meet you."

It was a short walk from the bar to the pier and onto a zodiac with an engine far too powerful for simply shuttling bodies between larger vessels moored in the harbor and the shore. As the pale Latina steered the vessel towards the deeper water of the outer moorings, Alex knew instinctively that they were headed for the yacht that had arrived the day before, the *Phoenix*. It had been in and out of the harbor for the last couple of years, and while not unusual to the point of gossip, no one knew anything about it, its crew, or its owner, either. It loomed large above them as they pulled alongside, and Alex tossed their bow line to a silent deck hand while the nameless woman cut the throttle.

Alex guessed the yacht measured at least ninety feet. Two more crewmen appeared on the fly deck of the bridge a story above him. Behind them sat a massive wheelhouse, and above it a Christmas tree of radar, sonar, and communications antennae. The vessel's beam was equally impressive, perhaps a third as wide as she was long. The low, exposed stern deck was big enough for a small jacuzzi and a fighting chair. Rod holders above Alex's head held fishing gear appropriate to the chair, as well as a host of smaller rigs. Warm light glowed from the entrance to the cavernous cabin. The blonde slid open a set of teak doors and gestured for him to enter.

"'Lo, Alex." The voice that came across the room was a rich baritone with more than a touch of humor in it. Alex found its source nestled in a leather chair inside the plush cabin. A decanter rested on a low table, midway through its duty to a pair of glasses amber with their charges.

"Jack Sweet. Hello."

Sweet's eyes glimmered in the cabin's light, much younger than the leathered skin, silvered hair, and chiseled chin that completed his face. His gestures were both confident and graceful, his piloting skills legendary.

"I knew you were good, but I didn't know it paid this well," Alex remarked, taking in the rest of the cabin. Forward of the sitting area a galley bar separated the cabin from a well-appointed kitchen, where a man with his back to Alex rummaged through the refrigerator. The blonde paced across the carpeted space and into the kitchen.

"It doesn't. Yet." Jack smiled at Alex and reached for his drink.

"Coors original, right?" The man in the kitchen handed a bottle to the blonde, who handed it to Alex across the galley table as he approached. Alex transferred it to his left and took the hand of the man in the kitchen. He noticed that the stranger wore his watch, a Vacheron Constantin no less, on his right hand. His grip was firm but not overbearing. He looked to be about forty, younger than Jack Sweet but older than Alex himself, and while elegantly groomed his face and hands showed signs of mileage.

"Right. Nice boat."

"Thank you. It is decidedly not cheap. The purchase price is only the beginning. Perhaps I should've listened to Sweet."

"That's right," Jack Sweet's baritone found them at the table. "If it flies, floats, or fucks, it's cheaper to rent." Alex laughed and the man joined him. The blonde did not.

"So it seems everyone knows each other, my drink preferences, and what the hell I'm doing here, except me."

"Well, you know Jack Sweet," the man offered.

"Everyone knows Sweet."

"And you can call me Kenny."

"Pleasure."

"Please, sit down."

The men settled into chairs next to Jack Sweet, the blonde disappeared down the staircase to the forward cabins, and Kenny regarded Alex as if considering a purchase.

"I've been watching you and Mercy for two years now."

"Why? We're not that exciting."

"Ah, but you have potential, kid. Do you ever think she's going to get back in the water?"

"I have no idea."

"Do you love her?"

"None of your business."

"Do you need her?"

"Kenny, thanks for the beer, but I don't need anyone. You going to give me a lift back to the pier or should I call a shoreboat?"

"Relax, Alex. Just wondering."

"Well, I'm tired of wondering. What's your angle?"

"How would you like to make half a million dollars for two days work?"

"Who do I have to kill?"

"No one."

"How long do I go to jail if I get caught?"

"True. Endeavors of this type are not exactly legal, but the risk is minimal and the reward, well, I guess you'll have to judge for yourself how much half a mil would mean to you and Mercy."

"I'm listening."

Jack Sweet tabled his drink and leaned forward in his chair. "Do you know how hard it is to smuggle something into the United States, Alex?"

"Smuggle what?"

"It doesn't matter. Anything."

"I'm not running guns or bombs if that's what you mean. That's murder by association."

"It's nothing like that," Kenny said. "Hell, guns aren't smuggled into the U.S. They're smuggled out. Mexican traffickers bring drugs and people into the country, and use the same tunnels and vehicles to smuggle guns into Mexico, which the cartels buy at top dollar with their ample cash supplies. Talk about a double payday. But there's far too much risk. Too many are caught, too many end up on the radar of the authorities, and too many kill each other. No, it's better to go all in once, and then move on."

"It doesn't look like you need the cash. Why do it at all?"

"Anyone of means will tell you that it takes tremendous income to even sustain wealth. Besides, this is a slam dunk, and it's exciting. To me, the action is the juice."

"So Sweet is telling me how hard it is to smuggle into the U.S., and you're telling me how easy it is. Great."

"It is easy, Alex. It will only work once, but that's enough. That's plenty."

"Listen, kid," Jack Sweet said. "It's incredibly difficult to smuggle into the United States. But how hard is it to move a package from here, from your little island, to the mainland?"

"Well," thought Alex, peering at the ceiling, "I wouldn't get on an Express Boat with anything hot. But you've got your own boat. If it never goes into international waters, just motors out here from the mainland and back, no one would raise an eyebrow. Hell, this is the most popular boating destination in the state. Sail home on a summer Sunday and you're one of hundreds. But how do you get your precious package here?" Alex's head snapped around as he leveled a stare at Jack Sweet. "You're shitting me. It can't be that simple."

"Most beautiful solutions are, my friend," said Kenny. "Einstein explained the known universe with three letters and one number."

Jack Sweet sipped his drink and licked his lips. "I'll be flying in from, ah, an undisclosed location. Kenny will have false flight plans logged that show me coming out of Santa Barbara, or L.A., or wherever, hell, it doesn't matter. No one at your tiny airport checks. I land. You move the package from the plane, down the hill into town, and it goes to the mainland without ever passing a cop."

"Why do you need me?"

"Because," Kenny said, "We are not quite brazen enough to do it ourselves right under the noses of the locals. An islander, however, enjoying an afternoon at the Airport in the Sky, and then, say, going for a dive afterward, wouldn't cause any suspicion whatsoever."

"Why the dive?"

"Again, because it just might raise a bit of suspicion if a bit of an unusual flight took place the same day that a bit of an unusual boat pulled out. All it takes is one call to the Coast Guard. So, the boat won't be here when the plane lands. No connection at all."

"I land," Sweet said. "You take the package into town. Just a few bags of laundry. Later, you and Mercy decide to go for a dive, just a few bags of dive gear with you. She'll know of a quiet, out of the way spot. Deep, protected water. We have a few ideas, but nobody knows the dive sites better than her. You take the packages down, watertight cases, and hide them on the bottom. No one sees, no one knows, no one is the wiser. They can sit there a week, a month, a year. Make sure there's no heat from the flight. When everything is cool, a short weekend boat trip to the island, another easy dive, a quick rendezvous with you, and you're rich."

"What's in the packages?"

"Alex, I'm surprised at you," Kenny said. "We've put a lot of time into evaluating you. You think you were just plucked out of a bar? You know the area, you move amongst the locals without arousing interest, you and Mercy have the dive end of it covered. We also thought that you shared our philosophies regarding such things, and wouldn't have a problem with it. If you do, then we've got a problem, indeed."

"What philosophies are those?"

Sweet filled his drink from the decanter and held it aloft. "Prohibition has never worked, Alex. Never has and never will. Is booze good for you? Does that stop people from drinking? What did making it illegal do? It made it more glamorous, more mysterious, more attractive. The government has obviously never heard of Blackbeard's closet or Pandora's box. What else did it do? It drove the prices through the fucking roof. It made booze worth as much as gold. It created a criminal empire. It made Al Capone the richest man in the country."

"You want to be Al Capone?"

"No, no," said Kenny. "We wish to exploit, for profit, for a social experiment, and maybe to make a goddamn point, the ignorance of prohibition. How much money can you make rum running these days? What's in the packages is valuable because, and only because, the government has its head stuck up its ass. That's fine with me as long as it stays there until we all get paid."

"I need to talk to Mercy."

"Naturally," said Kenny. "Allow me to suggest that you keep things, shall we say, theoretical, until you've gotten a feel for her reaction. No need to bring up specifics or names. May I remind you that we've had an eye on you for some time now, and it would be unwise to compromise anyone's position at this point."

"Understood. I'll tell you right now that it sounds good to me. Hell, I could-"

"Talk to Mercy, Alex," said Jack Sweet. "We'll give you a lift to shore."

Desert

Admiral Cavendish's cabin glowed with the surreal color of candlelight reflected in gold. His First Lieutenant moved from chest to chest, raising the lids, counting, quill scribbling figures and notes on parchment.

"These are our private records, Lieutenant." The Admiral's young face and thin mustache showed little emotion. Only his dark eyes betrayed joy.

"Or course, sir. We will compile an official list for inspection in England."

"This will keep those dogs on the *Content* quiet as well. They see none of the treasure until we return. We will decide a, fair, division when we are safely home."

The Lieutenant exchanged a knowing glance with his Admiral. "Yes, sir."

"Pull the vessel away from shore. Make sure Captain Edmund and his men clean up the mess on the beach."

"And what of the Spanish and their prisoners, sir?"

"Leave them here. If the *Content* wishes to spare some of her supplies for them, that is Captain Edmund's affair. We are now in charge of something more valuable."

"Yes sir."

-

In the prisoner's hold of the *Content*, Ina crouched in the corner of her cell. Rust flaked from iron bars sunk deep into the wooden planks, and the solid walls trapped the stale air as well as the Japanese prisoners. Sweat mixed with fear and permeated the cramped cabin. Three paces of bare deck separated the barred cell from an outer door.

Ina's lithe Japanese asked the brothers, "How did you come to be in my family's service?"

Akira smiled at her. "Our families have known each other for generations. Many loyalties strengthened and alliances formed when the Portuguese guns appeared. Japanese are killing Japanese with European fire."

"And Japanese steel."

"Are you paid to serve?" Perhaps Ina hime's rank allowed the rudeness of the question. But Akira did not shrink from her stare. Perhaps not.

"Not at present." And he smiled again.

Ina quietly observed the outer door. It opened. The two young Japanese men rose and stood over Ina, their backs to her, as Edmund advanced into the room and approached the bars.

"Leave her alone," the taller of the men said.

"Well, well, the King's tongue."

Ono, misunderstanding Edmund, said, "Yes. For King. Ina for great King. You must leave her alone."

"That explains it. Well, the Spanish King won't be receiving this particular gift."

Ina watched the exchange. "Akira," she whispered. The taller man knelt and she spoke hurriedly to him in Japanese.

"Ladies and gentlemen, this is not a committee," said Edmund, rattling the bars with the barrel of his pistol.

Akira straightened. "Sir, Ina knows of another, coin? Money? Another-"

"Treasure?"

"Yes, treasure. Secret. Your men did not find. On the boat."

"I burned your boat."

"Not our boat. Boat of pigs."

"I'm not particularly interested in your assessment of Spanish character, though to be honest I do agree with it."

Ina's Japanese again found its way to Akira's ear. He spoke to Edmund again.

"The treasure is there. Hidden below. Still there. Leave us alone. She will show you."

Edmund rattled the barrel of his pistol across the bars again, staring from Akira to Ina and back again. Then he backed to the outer door, withdrew, and closed it behind him.

-

The Navigator stood at the helm of the *Content* and watched the sun rise. The vessel remained at anchor, and the hull of the once proud *Santa Ana* still smoldered in the surf, burned to the water line. The Spaniards and their captives now found themselves thrown onto the same desolate beach. During the night they had retreated into the forest fringing the narrow beach and made makeshift camps.

Edmund appeared beside him and scanned the horizon. The *Desire* had cast off, and waited perhaps a quarter mile to sea. "I see nothing to lose."

"Sir?"

"Lower a boat. I'm going ashore."

"Sir?"

"Was I unclear?"

"No, sir. Yes, sir! Lower a longboat!" Sailors crawled from hatches, still groggy from sleep and bitter with misfortune. Some looked to the *Desire* and cursed.

"You're coming with me," Edmund barked. "Allow the men to return to their bunks once we are away."

"Yes, sir."

Edmund stood in the bow of the long boat, a length of chain wrapped around his fist. It snaked from his grip for several feet before terminating at a shackle on Ina's wrist. The young Japanese men were not chained. Edmund knew they would neither desert her nor attempt to overpower him with her life at stake. The Navigator bent to the oars, moving them steadily towards shore. Akira crouched between Ina and the Navigator, and looked steadily at Edmund.

"If this is a lie, you stay here with the Spanish, and she comes with me," he told the prisoners.

"She does not lie. Ever."

"How touching."

The Navigator rowed until the long boat's keel scraped bottom. At Edmund's gesture he and Akira leapt out and dragged the boat clear of the surf. Edmund stepped onto the wet sand and dragged Ina out after him. Akira caught her and helped her to her feet. Edmund withdrew a key from his jacket pocket and opened the shackle. Ina rubbed her wrist and looked sadly at Akira. Edmund stepped between them as the Navigator stood guard. "No lies. No tricks."

"And you, no lie?" She gazed levelly at him while Akira translated.

"My dear, first of all, you are speaking to an Englishman and an officer. Second, you have no choice." He backed next to the Navigator and raised his pistol to her chest.

"No treasure," was her response to the threat. Edmund chuckled and pivoted, leveling the musket at Akira.

"Just like the Spanish." Emotion crept into her voice for the first time. Edmund cocked the gun. She fixed him with the same stoic gaze for a moment, then spun about and made her way to the remains of the *Santa Ana*.

"I help her," Akira said.

"Not yet."

Ina fell once in the surf, then scrambled onto the wreckage of the galleon. Nothing but charred wood stood above the water line, and the receding tide began to reveal the ravaged hull. Fog licked at the remains of the once proud vessel. Ina threw blackened planks aside, and found the remains of a staircase. Her small frame disappeared below.

Edmund watched her go. "I changed my mind. If this is a trick, you both die."

"I tell you. No lie. She is no slave."

"The hell she isn't."

Ina reappeared and waved towards the beach.

"Please, we help her now."

Edmund nodded and Akira strode for the galleon. Edmund and the Navigator followed as far as the surf line, and then spread out along the length of the blackened hull, keeping watch. Ina and Akira disappeared below. Edmund glanced again at the *Desire*, waiting on the horizon. The fog grew thicker. Edmund glanced at his Navigator, and again to sea. The sound of creaking wood brought his attention again to the wreck. Akira and Ina reappeared, hefting a small chest between them. It looked to Edmund only large enough to hold perhaps two coconuts, yet the prisoners strained to haul it from the wreck and drop it at Edmund's feet.

"Open it."

"I give you the treasure, you leave us the chest. Leave us here." Akira translated as best he could.

"Don't make it hard on yourself. My men will tear this chest apart."

Ina smiled and shook her head. "No lie."

"No lie."

An ornate key appeared from the folds of Ina's haggard kimono. Edmund plucked it from her grasp and thrust it into the chest's lock. It would not yield.

"It will not work for you. I give you the treasure. You leave us here with the chest. It is the last I have from my family. Take the gold." Akira gestured as he spoke.

Edmund nodded. Ina knelt to the chest, touched the key, and the lid snapped open. Edmund and the Navigator drew closer as Ina opened the chest. An unearthly glow lit the four faces.

"Indeed." Edmund closed the lid of the chest gently, withdrew the key, and slipped it into a deep pocket. "It will work for me. Back to the ship. And, before I forget my manners, thank you." Edmund snapped the shackle back around Ina's wrist and chained her to the chest.

Akira began to protest and Ina stopped him with a gesture. She bent and grasped the chest. Akira took the opposite side and they struggled it down the beach and into the longboat. Edmund put his arm around his Navigator and walked behind. He whistled tunelessly and watched the fog blow in.

Onboard the *Content*, Edmund saw the prisoners secured below. Everything he desired from this voyage now lay chained, locked in his hold, on his vessel. He watched the anchor drawn from the shallow bottom with the sweat of his men. He felt his ship rise and wake as the men secured the anchor and set sail. Wisps of fog made their way over the deck and amongst the sailors.

"Navigator, set a course north."

"Sir, our flagship is due west."

"I said north."

"Sir, respectfully, we will lose the *Desire* in this fog if we are not careful, sir."

"Exactly. Head north."

The Navigator stared blankly at his captain for a moment. Then resolution crept across his face. "Come about. New course - north!" The men exchanged glances and then rushed to obey. Sails snapped, dropped, billowed, and pivoted at their hands' commands. Some sailors appeared bewildered, others smiled. One caught Captain Edmund's eye and snapped to attention, saluting, and grinning. Edmund returned the salute and the sailor sprang back to work, his expression never changing.

The Mexican Fisherman

Mercy and Alex sat on the pier, watching the sun rise from the ocean. What began as a blueblack line between water and air shifted to a soft glow before painting fire across the surface of the sea. It found deepening lines at the corners of Mercy's eyes as she looked from it to Alex.

"I'm sorry about the job. I missed you last night," she said. He did not respond, just stared at one of the yachts on an outer mooring. "Elbows has an idea about the coin."

"Look, Mercy, I don't think that coin is going to amount to anything more than what it is - an interesting relic. Put it on the mantle and make up a tall tale to go along with it."

"You're serious."

"Never let the truth get in the way of a good story. It's just a random coin. The ocean blows shit around constantly. Things have hit the drink in Denmark and been found off New York, for crissakes. And even if there is something down there, it's no way to get rich. For every successful treasure hunt you hear about, hundreds of millions are poured into the water with nothing, absolutely nothing coming back. Find a treasure hunting company on the stock exchange for me. And even if, even if, that one in a billion chance hits and somebody finds something, all of a sudden the governments of six goddamn countries are crying 'thief!' and insisting they still own something they stole from somebody else hundreds of years ago. The guys who actually made the find die while it works its way through the courts. Maybe somebody's grandkid gets a few bucks for college, and the bureaucrats pat themselves on the back all the way to the museum."

"Alex, it's not about getting rich. It's about closing a circle in my life. Something, I don't know, something powerful, something important, something I don't understand started all of this two years ago."

"It was an accident. Some guy took you home, then you took him diving, and he fucked up. That's it. I've been telling you that for months. Listen to me. You want to get back in the water? We have a chance to make some real money, and all it takes is a couple of dives. Remember Jack Sweet?"

"You know something? The past few weeks I've felt like you're not listening to me anymore. And you want to know what that makes me wonder? It makes me wonder if you ever did."

"Alright, alright. I'm listening." Still he stared at the yacht. Mercy followed his gaze. The early light blazed across the water and sent tongues of red and green light dancing across its stern. She could not make out the vessel's name.

"Alex, I just want to be happy."

"That's what I'm talking about. Imagine never having to work again."

"I want to tell you a story. My cousin told it to me after the tsunami almost killed him. No one knows who wrote it, or if it really happened, but it's been around awhile for a reason."

"I'm enthralled already." He chuckled. "Okay, okay, I'm listening."

"There once was a Mexican fisherman who lived in a small town by the sea. Each day he would rise with the sun and go in search of fish. He was both skilled and lucky and usually returned with a good catch."

"Sounds good to me. Half a mil goes far in Mexico."

"I'm telling you a story. Then you can tell me one." Alex quieted and she continued. "He would then have dinner with his wife and play with his children before putting them to bed. Sometimes he would go to the local cantina for a beer with friends in the band."

"Cheesy."

"Shut up."

"Okay."

"One night at the bar an American businessman sat down next to him and said, 'I have heard you are the best fisherman in town. I will pay you to take me fishing tomorrow.' He made a generous offer and the Mexican agreed."

"Back on track."

"The next day was good and they caught many fish. That night they returned to the cantina. 'You have a rare gift, and an exceptional opportunity,' said the American."

"Ocean, fishing, money. Touchdown," Alex smiled.

Mercy continued, "'What is this opportunity?' asked the Mexican. 'You can start a business, take tourists fishing, and turn a handsome profit.' 'And what will I do with the money?'

The American advised his ignorant friend, 'Invest it. Buy more boats, hire crews, make more money, and grow rich.' 'What shall I do when I become rich?''

Alex, unable to contain himself, blurted out, "That's the point. You can do whatever you want!"

Mercy shushed him. "'With many years of hard work, my Mexican friend, you can retire. Then you can do anything you want. What will you do?' The American asked."

"Now we're talking."

"'I would like to go fishing every day. Then I want to have dinner with my wife, play with my kids, and perhaps have a beer with my friends in the band.'"

"Christ. I see."

"Do you? It's not all about the money. And there are only three ways to get a lot of money, Alex. Inherit it, earn it or steal it. That's it."

"Who cares where it comes from?

"I don't know what Jack Sweet told you last night, and you don't seem to give a damn what Elbows told me."

"What did he tell you?"

"He thinks the coin came from a Spanish Galleon. He thinks it was captured by English privateers, that's why it's this far north. He thinks there's an entire wreck down there, an English wreck, loaded with Spanish treasure."

"I keep telling you, it's one in a billion, and even if there is, you'll never see a dime of it. You'll get a thank you card from a museum."

"And I keep trying to tell you, it's not about getting rich. It's about-"

"Goddamn it, Mercy. Yes it is." He stood and walked away from her down the pier.

Japan 16th Century

It was explained to Ina from a young age that her life was not her own. As a child she padded through the serenity of her father's garden, listening to the muffled clinking of the peasant's tools as they worked the soil, and the whisperings of her mother, painting a picture of beauty and service. The Japanese she used was ancient, delicate, comforting, and powerful.

"You are to be tended, by me and my servants, as these are tended," her mother said, pointing to the delicate trees and silken petals. You do not belong to this house, this soil, or to me any more than these plants do. This is a place to grow, and rest, and learn, and blossom. When the time is right and you are beautiful and dutiful enough, you will be given to a man, as I was to your father. Then, it will be your turn to plant your garden, raise your children, and bring your beauty into the world."

Ina began to cry, and her mother gave her an embrace that was both a comfort and a warning. "You must be stronger than that," she admonished. "There is much to learn in these gardens, and nothing to fear, as long as you do as you are told."

From that moment on she lived with a sense of resignation. As she grew and outpaced the beauty of every other living thing on the substantial grounds, her parents were pleased. This increased the weight of her sorrow. She studied dutifully, learning proper speech, etiquette, reading and writing. Her pen was beautiful, too, but seldom was she allowed to write her own thoughts. Open to critique and censure, she kept her own writing private, sharing only glowing praise for the works of past masters and whatever had created the natural beauty around her.

The duties to learn were many. In the Japanese nobility, it was the woman's job to run the household, raise and educate the children, oversee the crops and gardens and peasants, and, Ina was told one day, revenge the murder of her husband, if necessary. Still, it was both a rare and brief time of peace in her country's history, though soon the Portuguese landed and the diamyo went to war again with the swords that spit fire and killed from the other side of the battlefield, and everything changed.

Ina had thought, and in hindsight she believed her parents had thought as well, that she would go to one of the neighboring daimyo or the son of a daimyo. She had accepted her eventual uprooting from the home she knew and loved, and had intentionally kept the warm embrace of her home and family at a distance, knowing one day she would be taken from it. She remembered the day she first bled, and her surprise and horror, and the surprise of her mother that it had happened so young, and then her mother's comforts that she was not dying. She believed her mother, believed that she was not dying, not then, but with the sudden shock of adolescent realization, it occurred to her for the first time that one day she would, indeed, die. This threw her into conflict, for if she had kept her own home at a distance, knowing she would be taken from it, how was she to face life knowing the same fate would return to take her again? She saw the bravery with which her mother faced the same world, though already past the first taking, and closer to the second. She saw the bravery of her father and the daimyo when the firearms began to appear and the peace ended. She was taught that courage was honorable and believed it, but secretly she knew that it was something more. Bravery was the only way to live in such a world and not die immediately in misery and despair. This personal philosophy made her as strong as she was beautiful and her parents were proud. She thought they would be horrified if they knew the source of her valiance. Then, one day, it didn't matter anymore.

-

"Come, it is time to show you something." Ina's mother stood over her as she sat in the garden. She was supposed to have been pruning the young bonsai, but was merely stroking them slowly and peering across the rolling land to where it met the sky. Her mother took her hand, lifting her to her feet, and Ina fell in behind her, matching her silent strides as her mother led her to a small temple. As they slipped from their cloth shoes and entered, the faintest trace of incense wafted outside and rose into the sky.
"You have been dutiful, if a bit of a daydreamer. Your speech and ettiquite are excellent. Your pen will be better once you abandon your own stories and focus on the beauties of the masters and of nature."
"I am to have no-"
"You are to have many responsibilities, which will require all of your time and attention."
"As yours do here, mother." It was not a question.
"Precisely. But your father has greater plans for you. You are worthy of a prince."
"And this means?"

"That if you practice dutifully enough, and manage to lose the willfulness with which you persist, you will one day be a princess."

Ina's eyes raised to the rafters of the temple. The modest walls served only to keep the wind out and serenity in. "Why are we here?"

"Our family has guarded something of great value for centuries. Your father has seen to its safekeeping, and his father before him, and his..." As she spoke she moved to an alcove concealing several large chests. While not ornate, the quality of the wood and the dovetail joints belied both a quiet beauty and strength. A guard passed by an open window above the chests. He looked inside, the top of his spear disappearing behind the wall, and nodded respectfully.

Ina knelt before the largest of the chests and ran her fingers over its smooth, patient surface.

"It must contain great wealth."

"Do not judge hastily." Ina watched as her mother withdrew a small brass key from her robe and opened the chest. She peered silently inside. A golden splash played across her face as she inhaled.

"I have never seen such things."

"They don't matter. They are intended to catch the eye of the ignorant. Here..." Her mother reached inside the chest, and the golden play of light continued as Ina heard objects slide against the bottom of the chest. From the corner of the big chest her mother pulled a smaller chest, perhaps large enough to hold two coconuts. The woman strained against its weight despite its diminutive size.

"This is the true treasure, and the true secret. Look now, for we will not open it again. Once you understand the secret, which will come with the passing years, you will know its true value."

A second key appeared from within the confines of the larger chest, and with a click and a groan as old as time the smaller chest opened. Before, the play of golden light in the room was nothing more than firelight catching gold. The light that poured forth from the small chest was a color Ina had never seen before, and could not even describe. It held a life of its own, not a reflection, but an entity. Her mother reached into the chest and withdrew a gold coin. The glow caught it.

"It is the color of the sea after a storm," Ina said. Her mother handed her the coin. "The coin is not Japanese, mother."

"No, no, it shouldn't even be in the same house. Some Japanese trade with the Portugese and the Spanish. This is their gold, and they crave it more than anything. We have filled the chest with it, and the larger chest, as camouflage. Should it ever fall into the wrong hands, we can use the gold to barter, and preserve the true treasure." With that, her mother returned the coin to the chest, lowered the lid reverentially, and locked it.

"You will have the key when you are old enough. You will take it with you if you are to be princess, and you will guard it and teach your family the secret."

"What is the secret?"

"Not yet, little one." She raised her hand to her daughter's heart. "Yet it is as much here," and moved her hand to the chest, "as here."

"I don't understand."

"That is as it should be, for now. But there is something more you must understand."

Ina fixed her mother with a puzzled gaze as a delicate knife appeared from the folds of the elder's kimono.

"It is called a kaiken. The blade was forged before your great grandfather was born. It was folded and hammered exactly twenty times, which created one million layers of steel. Never touch the edge."

"It glows like the chest."

"It is from a similar fire. The world is not as kind a place as you would believe from the life you have known thus far. Precious things must be guarded. This is to remind you of that." The bone handle pivoted into Ina's hand, warm against her skin.

"In some families, young women receive a kaiken on their wedding day. Because of who you are, and what we guard, you may need yours before then. Never be without it. You will learn to carry it safely concealed. You will learn it as a tool, a weapon, and a companion. Your new training begins tomorrow."

-

Three years later Ina remembered the touch of her mother's fingers on her kimono as she pressed her own hand against her heart and peered at the plumes of smoke on the horizon. A low thundering reached her ears, and she heard dull pops and larger explosions echo from the hills and into her chest. Her mother appeared from the temple and rushed towards her. Two swordsmen trailed her, their friendly, frightened eyes fixed on Ina.

"They promised they wouldn't attack," she growled.

"There is no time to think of justice, my child. Our daimyo are defeated. We are no match for the guns. You must flee." The swordsmen each took one of Ina's elbows, and her mother led them to the temple. Their swords scraped the wood of the doorframe as they disappeared inside with her mother, and reemerged a moment later with the small chest between them.

"Take the key, my child." As Ina pressed the key into the folds of her gown, her mother's arms enveloped her and she felt a single wet drop splash into her hair. "This is Akira, and this Ono. They will protect you. Should you be overrun, use the gold to trade for freedom, and protect this at all costs. Do not lose it, and above all do not let the invaders have it. It will help you in times of need, and give you light in times of darkness." The clash of steel and the boom of arquebuses and cannons interrupted her. Then new sounds reached Ina's ears, and she realized it was something she had never heard before, the sound of men screaming.

"Hurry now. Remember what you have learned. Remember that I love you, and never forget what true value is."

Ina kissed her mother's cheek. A horse drawn wagon rolled a cloud of dust over and between them. Ina found herself in the small, open bed of the wagon with the chest beside her, underneath a thin layer of straw. Ono leapt onto the front of the wagon and grabbed the reins. Another horse appeared underneath Akira and they began to gallop away. As her mother stood and watched them go, more smoke poured over the hills and began to envelop her. Ina peered into her eyes with a quiet, placid stare that held no weakness, until the distance and the smoke obscured her completely.

Gambling at the Casino

Alex found Lucky Tom at Casino Point, watching instructors conduct dives from shore. For decades scuba divers congregated at the narrow strip of breakwater between the famous building and the ocean. Just outside the harbor, the point offered calm, shallow water for training, as well as a sloping bottom leading to lush kelp forests and even a few wrecks. Recently the City of Avalon installed a concrete staircase and steel railings leading into the sea, just like a swimming pool. It made entrances and exits while wearing heavy scuba gear beautifully simple, and made the point quite possibly the best shore diving location in the state.

The most famous building on the island stood behind them, the iconic Casino. Its twelve circular stories of art deco aplomb overlooked the harbor and point since 1929. As Alex thrust his hands into his jeans and stared up at the cream colored pillars and archways defining the grand ballroom on the top floors, and the round red roof covering all, Tom approached him from behind.

" You know, at least once a year someone asks me where the slot machines are," said Lucky Tom.

"That's happened to me, too."

"One time I was out here and a couple actually came up carrying plastic cups full of quarters." Tom grinned.

"I bet you figured out a way to get the quarters," said Alex, and Lucky Tom's grin grew wider.

"Casino is actually an old Italian word for 'meeting place' or something like that. There has never been any gambling." Tom's eyes turned to watch the divers. "I think it was old man Wrigley's idea of a joke, especially considering the carousing that accompanied the roaring twenties."

"Bet the Depression didn't do business any good."

"That's why you always cover your ass, kid."

"Why?" Alex asked.

"Because no one else will." Tom slopped sun screen on his bald head and stuck the tube back in the pocket of his board shorts.

Alex turned and watched the water. "Why are you out here, Tom?"

"I'm watching instructors from the mainland train divers."

"Why?"

"Because a good instructor who has been well trained, knows the local waters, knows the thick wetsuits, the weights, the kelp, is worth his weight in gold."

"And?"

"And an incompetent or inexperienced instructor, or one who is only used to the Caribbean, can be dangerous."

"Tom, I didn't know you cared."

"I do. About myself and my business. First, you've got to realize that scuba diving has become extremely safe."

"Yeah," said Alex, "I've seen that t-shirt you sell. 'Remember when sex was safe and scuba diving was dangerous?'"

"Exactly. Statistically, the sport with the accident incidence closest to diving is bowling. The most dangerous thing these guys do is drive to the Express Boat. By far. But when accidents do happen, or when somebody screws up, it can be serious."

"Simply because it's underwater. You can't just stop, like hiking or getting off a bicycle," said Alex.

"Right. And there's a big difference between diving for fun and training. See, when certified divers have an accident, it's on them. That's what happened to Mercy. That kid with her was certified, and had his own gear. No one knows for sure what happened down there, except him, and he's not talking. But my shop held no liability. They were just buddies on a fun dive. All they were using of mine was my air, and my air is clean. No lawsuit.

"But if a shop and instructor gets someone who isn't certified, a student, hurt or killed, it's bad all around. Bad for the industry. Bad for tourism. Bad for business."

"And bad for the dead student."

"I suppose so."

"Like Mercy says, you're all heart, Tom."

"You can take it any goddamn way you want, kid. No one gets hurt under my name. My instructors are checked out thoroughly - by me - regardless of what their résumé says. My gear is always serviced. My records are complete. I'm thorough. I'm safe. For selfish reasons. Some of these jokers scare me."

"Why?"

"If the instructor doesn't know these waters, if the gear isn't serviced properly, even if the gear is serviced but there aren't records of it, you've got a major liability problem. If something happens and the lawyers can prove that things weren't right when the student entered the water, it can turn into criminal liability. No level of limited liability corporations or red tape can protect the shop or the owner then. People can go bankrupt, even go to jail. And even if it's somebody else's ass in jail, my business suffers. What most dive shops don't realize is that the other dive shops are not the enemy."

"Who's the enemy, Tom?"

"The golf pros. The surf shops. The mountain bikes. The alternate activities. We make far more money if we cooperate, and especially if we're safe. It's the only way."

"So where are your instructors?"

"We've got them all on the boat today. Big trip."

"Sounds like maybe you could use Mercy." Alex shot Lucky Tom a glance as he spoke. Tom turned to face him.

"Is that why you're out here, kid?"

"Actually, no. About Mercy, I'm not sure-"

"You're not sure you can use her anymore."

"What the hell is that supposed to mean?"

"It means you've got to look out for yourself, kid."

"Why did you fire her?"

"None of your damn business. If she wants to know, she can come and ask. Always nice to see her."

"She didn't send me out here, Tom."

"Then why are you here?"

"I'm thinking about a new business deal. You seem to have the best head for business, so I thought I'd have a chat with you."

"Cool. What is it and what's my cut?"

"Your cut is nothing, and I can't talk about what it is. I just need-"

"You need?"

"I don't know..."

"Theoretical advice, kid?"

"I suppose so."

"Ok, kid, here is your free theoretical advice. It's the only thing you're ever going to get for free from me. And that should tell you what it's worth."

Alex looked at Lucky Tom. "I'm listening."

"No one and nothing in this world gives two shits for you. You must do what is best for you. Not Mercy, not your mamma, you. There is no God watching over you, and there is no heaven and no hell waiting for you. This is all you get. And the only one who cares what you get is you."

"Mercy told me you said something like that once. Most people belive in God."

"Most people are superstitious, and so self-absorbed that they actually believe there is an omniscient, omnipresent, benevolent creator of the universe, that not only has the time to listen to the prayers of six billion selfish human beings, but gives a sufficient shit to act upon them. People pray for rain, people pray over the outcome of a basketball game. You telling me the creator of the universe not only exists but is a Lakers fan?"

"I don't know. I pray..."

"When?"

"When I..."

"When you need something or want something. You sit around until that works out for you."

"That's pretty harsh, Tom."

"You need to read some Dawkins. The problem with believing in a creator is simple. Who created the creator? It's a problem of infinite regress. Think about it. I tried being open minded. I tried listening to people look around at the beauty and the structure in the world, and attribute it to a kind God."

"What's wrong with that, Tom? How can you argue against that? You telling me all this is random?"

"It's not random, kid. It's evolved. The intelligent design folks argue that the world, the universe, is so complex that something must have created it. Look at a bird's wing, the solar system, your own circulatory system, whatever."

"It sure looks engineered."

"Fine. So you argue that it is so complex it must have been engineered. That assumes a creator sufficiently complex to... create really complex things. Then that creator must be complex, which begs the question..."

"Who created the creator?"

"Right. The argument falls flat on its face by its own defining principles. Now, I can give you a million examples of complex things evolving from simple things. In fact, it is the only way in the known world that complex things come to be. No God, kid. Survival of the fittest. Your circulatory system is complex because all of the trillions of organisms that have come before you evolved increasingly complex systems over millenia, while most of them died out. Your heart, your brain, you, exist because of the competition of organisms. The orgin of species occurs as a direct, irrefutable function of survival of the fittest. It's the only way it makes any sense."

"What if you're wrong?"

"That was Pascal's argument."

"The mathematician?" asked Alex.

"Hey, not bad, kid. Yes."

Just then a splash came from the stairs leading into the sea.

"Look at that," Lucky Tom said. "That instructor put his students in the water first. He was still standing on the stairs while they got in. They don't have their masks on, they don't have their regulators in their mouths. If anything happens, if one isn't positively buoyant, if a goddamn wave breaks, they can't see, they can't breathe, and the dumb ass is on the stairs with his fins in his hands. He can't help them."

"But they're floating just fine."

"Yes. Which is why I'm not over there kicking ass. But what if they weren't? What if something goes wrong? Too many assholes in this line of work assume nothing is going to happen. I assume that something is. Prevention is ninety percent of this business, kid."

"Well, he's in the water with them now. Looks like they live another day."

"The maddening thing about this sport is that it's so safe if you do it right. Don't get me wrong, anyone can have an accident. You can get killed walking your doggie. But most of the time if there's an issue, it's operator error. Period."

"What about Pascal? The mathemetician must've argued against God."

"Nope, kid. For him. And he used math. Sort of."
Alex just stared at Lucky Tom until he continued.

"Pascal's argument goes like this: Alex believes in
God. Tom doesn't. If Tom is right, both lead their lives,
both die. Game over. Alex spends some time in church
when he could be drinking and fucking, but essentially it's a
wash. Now case number two. Alex is right. Tom goes to
hell and endures endless suffering. Alex goes to heaven and
gets a shiny new harp. Mathematically it makes sense to
believe in God. If you're wrong it costs you nothing, if
you're right, you get salvation over damnnation."

"Wow."

"Yeah. But what I have a problem with is the
concept of an all-knowing, all-powerful creator that doesn't
make any evolutionary sense whatsoever, that exists
nonetheless, and in his omnipotence is preoccupied with
whether you believe in him or not. It's ridiculous. I created
the universe, and what I care about most is whether Alex
believes in me. So Alex pretends to believe in me because
he's scared of what will happen if he doesn't? How noble.

"Further, how do you know you've got the right
God? All the Jews, Muslims, Catholics in the world think
you're going to hell because you've got the wrong God or
are praying to the wrong statue. So you must you believe, or
feign belief, because you're scared of what dreams may
come when we have shuffled off this mortal coil. You also
have to be sure you pick the right God. You think Islam is
just as ridiculous as I do. Some illiterate seventh century
preacher tells you it's okay to beat your wives, kill a woman
for having sex out of wedlock, and it's the word of God?
Ridiculous."

"That is ridiculous, Tom."

"And how about the Jews? Got any tattoos?"

"Yeah, this tribal band." Alex pulled up the sleeve of his t-shirt and showed Lucky Tom his bicep.

"No salvation for you, according to the Jews."

"That's silly. That has nothing to do with-"

"See that?" Tom, pointed to the sun, directly overheard.

"Yeah."

"I put sunscreen on because that's Apollo's chariot, drawn by firey steeds, and if he gives someone else the reins it will come too close to earth and burn my beautiful skull. That's not a ball of hydrogen that will one day die out and with it all life on Earth. That's a flaming chariot."

"That was disproven centuries ago, but I do dig mythology."

"See, we agree about how ridiculous every religion in the history of the world is, except yours. Imagine that."

"Ok. What if you're wrong? And how does this translate into your free theoretical advice?" Alex looked at the skinny bald man.

"You can shout down into the firey pit from the pearly gates and tell me how full of shit I was. In the meantime, I look out for myself. I do what's best for myself. In my line of work, that often means doing what's best, what's safest, for other people too. But don't ever kid yourself, Alex. I do it for me. No one and nothing else. Lucky Tom. Goddamn right. Nothing takes more planning or preparation than good luck. Pascal got that part right. Luck favors the prepared mind. Whatever you're thinking about doing, do what's best for you. Don't let anyone or anything get in your way. It is survival of the fittest. Period."

"Thanks, Tom. I think."

"Now get lost. Here comes that wanker with his students again. One doesn't have enough weight to descend and he didn't take any extra with him or use a descent line. See how he's also swimming in front of them? He can't even see his own students. If one went under right now, he wouldn't even know. Jesus Christ."

Alex laughed at the invocation.

"Right. Do what's best for you, Alex."

"I will." Alex shook Tom's hand and began to walk back to town. Tom pulled his phone from his pocket and swiped his finger across the screen.

"And I'll do what's best for me."

Undressing Cassiopeia

Alex and the Señora stood in the dark on the roof of the Aurora Hotel. Behind them Mediterranean style houses climbed slowly up the steep hills of the valley. More scattered around the hotel and down into the flats of the town. In front of them the harbor rested in a gentle curve. Cool and quiet in the calm of winter, only a few boats bobbed beneath their lights. The *Phoenix* had long since departed, and the Señora's room at the Aurora was booked another night.

"Sweet arrives tomorrow," she said.

"I'm ready."

"And you're certain you can secure the packages without Mercy?"

"Yes, and I'm damn sure they wouldn't be secure with her."

"Do you miss her?"

"She doesn't even know I'm gone."

"Really? You have an interesting take on women, my friend."

"I see a problem with the women who visit this island, and with the country in general."

"You mean apart from all the other men?" She was just a whisper too strong to be lithe and spent little time on her knees and less on her heels. But they needed Alex, so she indulged him. "I'm listening."

"The problem is the pretty ones are stupid and the cool ones are ugly."

"For the most part, true."

"You agree?!"

"Of course. It is also equally true that it's your fault."

"It's my fault chicks are either ugly or stupid?"

"Yes. That's why when you find someone with looks and personality, you're supposed to hold on to them. Some men don't realize how lucky they are, and fewer still even get that chance at all."

"You're talking about Mercy again," Alex sighed.

"I think you know that you two were never compatible. She was never the same after the accident, and you took advantage of that. That is why you are compatible with our team. But that has nothing to do with the fact that the abyss between women's looks and their personalities is the fault of men."

"How do you figure?"

"You guys let the beauty queen skate on her looks. She is never challenged to develop an intellect or a sense of humor, to say nothing of character. All she has to do is giggle and fuck and be beautiful, so that's all she does."

"And…" now he saw it and it was fun to play the straight man.

"And you're hard wired to ignore ugly chicks. It's not your fault. You've had it since childhood. I've read a great deal about your country, my friend. I saw a study with two different substitute teachers in elementary school classrooms. Both were actually graduate students at

Columbia. Both read the same story in the same tone to multiple elementary classes, posing as their substitute teacher. Upon return of the real teacher, the kids were asked to voice their opinions and preferences regarding the subs, and the responses were taped. Across the board, both boys and girls said the attractive sub was 'nice,' and 'good,' and 'pretty,' while the homely, overweight sub was 'mean,' and 'scary,' and 'big,' reading the same story the same way."

"Damn. Little kids."

"Yeah."

"Boys and girls."

"See, an unattractive girl is ignored. She has to be smart and witty and cool or she dies on the vine. It's not exclusive to the U.S. by any means, but especially here, hot chicks are often stupid and unattractive women are usually super cool and it's almost always guys' fault."

"Sorry. Mercy once told me the problem with adolescence in men..."

"What?"

"It lasts the rest of our lives."

Another laugh and another smoke and another beer. Alex gestured to the sky.

"Look, Scorpio."

"Where?" she asked as she turned away and backed into him.

"Three vertical," with a karate chop and a hand on her hip and then cheek to cheek with "and the curve of the tail."

"Of course."

"And here..." as he spun her gently North, "Cassiopeia."

"Looks like a 'W'."

"She's sitting in a chair. See the faint stars?"

"OK."

"And sometimes she's upside down. The Greeks saw this as a sign of shame. Hence the myth."

"Which god did she piss off?"

"Poseidon. The Sea God."

"Whoops."

"No shit. Just ask Mercy."

"How'd she manage that?"

"Mercy or Cassiopeia?"

"I know what happened to Mercy. Tell me about Cassiopeia."

"She boasted she was as beautiful as his sea nymphs."

"What were they called?"

"Shit." He paused and thought. "The Nereids."

"How do you know that?"

"Oh they beam the stuff out all over the place. You just gotta know how to grab it."

"You like mythology, Alex?"

"It's only beautiful because it's true."

"You plan it." Sip. "What did he do to punish Cassiopeia?"

"Nothing."

"Right."

"No, really, he made someone else do something to her."

"Of course. So like a God. Or a man."

"He sent a sea monster to terrorize her people. Cassiopeia's husband, the King, was told by an oracle that the only way to spare the city was to sacrifice their daughter to Poseidon. The King duly took his daughter to the shore and chained her to a rock. Thanks, Mom."

"What happened?"

"Perseus, fresh back from beheading Medusa, showed his trophy to the monster-"

"What was its name?"

"Bitch."

"Thought I didn't notice." Sip.

"Cetus."

"Kraken?"

"Nope. That was 'Clash of the Titans.' You learned your mythology from TV."

"And my English."

"So he turned the Cetus to stone and rode off with the girl."

"I wonder if she was beautiful or ugly. Smart or stupid. Skinny or fat."

"That's funny. Matter of perspective, I guess. Hell, for millennia, to the old school guys, Botticelli and Dore, beauty wasn't skinny. The girls had everything."

"What was the girl's name?" It took but a shuffle and a final point to the sky. "Andromeda."

And the necks gave in. A short while later they parted.

"You sure you're ready for tomorrow, Alex?"

"Yes." He knew when to shut up.

"How about tonight?" And she led him from the roof to her room.

The One Eyed Dragon

Ina bounced helplessly in the back of the rickety wagon. Ono cut a rapid pace down a little used path, ever lower, towards the sea. The leather cut into his hands as he alternately reined the rapidly tiring horse in or let her black flanks stretch and trot as the switchbacks in the trail dictated. Akira's brown steed loped along side, breathing easier with no wagon load to bear. Akira scanned the horizon, one hand on his reins, the other on the handle of his sword.

Ono turned his head and peered over his shoulder into the back of the wagon. "When we have left the plateau, we will skirt around the small fishing village on the coast. That is where the foreigners land to trade. Further to the south are daimyo sympathetic to your plight. We will find you shelter and keep the chest safe. I promise."

"And my family?"

"It is time to look at the road ahead, Ina hime," said Ono.

Ina rose from the back of the open wagon, bracing herself against the wooden planks as the wheels bumped over the rocky trail. She swung herself over the seat and plopped down next to Ono.

"Then it would only be proper to face front, yes?"

Ono managed a weak smile. "Of course, Princess," he said as he watched Akira watch the horizon. "I can smell the sea. We are almost down."

The bouncing wagon tried to buck the tiny wells of salty water from Ina's eyes, but she silently refused. When I am alone, she told herself. When I am alone.

The trio rounded a last bend in the trail and the sea appeared before them, shimmering in the cool light and stubborn breeze. Ina knew the water was far colder than it appeared, and she looked forward to having the village behind her and the chest secured with allies to the south.

A dull smacking thud erupted from the withers of Akira's horse. Blood exploded from it's shoulders, neck, and nostrils as a hollow boom reached them from the edge of a small stand of cherry trees. Akira looked down in astonishment at the blood pouring over his legs as the animal tried to rear, then crashed to the earth, throwing Akira into the grass at the trail's edge.

From the grove four horsemen appeared. One leveled a blunderbuss at the group as he approached. Two carried spears pointed the same direction. The fourth struggled to reload his musket as his horse trotted along with his fellows. As they approached Ina saw the leader scowl at her from behind his loaded gun. As he neared, the scowl turned into a squint, then she realized she was looking into the face of a daimyo or a young samurai with only one good eye. It ran over her in cold appraisal. No cruel passion, no preamble to rape and murder. It was the eye of a go player deciding which stones to take, the eye of a man who does not want material, but the land that lies beneath it. The other eye lolled lazily in its socket, yellow with the remnants of disease. It was impossible to tell what, if anything, it saw.

Ono's sword was already out when Akira leapt to his feet. The hiss of his steel accompanied his words. "Today is a good day to die. Don't you agree?"

"No." The young warrior appraised Akira with the same vulture eye.

"Then you owe me a horse."

"No. The ball was supposed to hit your leg and the horse. You owe my man thanks for sparing your leg with his poor aim."

"What do you want?"

"Your valuables and your girl. She will not be harmed. I have no interest in her." From the ice in his stare, Ina actually believed him.

"Not while we breathe." Akira planted his feet in the dust and raised his sword.

"You do not see the situation clearly. I killed your horse from across the road. You will die before you are close enough to smell the fire that killed you." Akira stood defiant in his motionlessness. "I see your life will not persuade you. That makes the decision simple tactically. Drop your sword-"

"Never-"

"Or I kill her." And the black eye of the barrel trained itself on Ina.

The raiding party drew lengths of rope from their saddle bags and bound Akira's arms behind him. The leader plucked Akira's katana from the grass and ran his eye down the length of the blade. The other lolled back towards the heavens as the young samurai grinned and spoke heavily, spittle landing on the blade.

"Such beautiful craftsmanship. Such artistry. Such uselessness now."

He pulled the saya, the wooden scabbard, from Akira's waist, wiped and then sheathed the blade.

"Still, it will bring a good price in trade." He handed it to his second, a sallow fellow already holding Ono's sword.

"The world has changed, my friend. I will release you after we complete our business, and I suggest you use this as a lesson. And what have we here?" The vulture eye found the chest underneath its woeful covering of hay.

"Gold," said Ina. She fingered the dagger in the folds of her kimono, but the black eyes of the guns stayed her hand.

"Excellent."

The ride to the small fishing village lasted but a few minutes. Akira and Ono bounced unceremoniously in the back of the wagon, their arms tight behind them. Ina had been bound as well, though with her hands in front. Perhaps this modest show of decency meant there was some way to salvage the disaster unfolding, Ina thought.

When the group approached the village, Ina saw peasants busying themselves with racks of fish, mending boats, and coiling lines. Above them and an arrow's flight to sea sat the largest ship she had ever seen. A constant flow of smaller boats made their way from shore to the galleon and back, and with each trip the galleon hunkered lower in the water.

Their captor rode ahead while one of his spearmen slowed the wagon. The other stood behind them, leading his companion's mount, and the other musketeer remained at a distance where he could kill but not be touched himself. Akira thought, the world is indeed changing. It is becoming poisoned.

The young samurai returned, the vulture eye fixed on the chest. Behind him rode a Spaniard, the first Ina had ever seen. She saw naturally pale skin worn dark and rough by the sun and sea. She saw metal everywhere, on his cap, his clothes, his weapons, his shoes, so many things she had never seen before. And she saw the cruelty in his eyes, and it was a cruelty of possession, of conquest, that she had seen before and would again.

Their captor tried to communicate with the Spaniard. He pointed to the chest, to Ina, and spoke in an increasingly loud voice. His Japanese became no more intelligible to the Spaniard as the volume increased. Despite her fear, Ina found this funny.

Akira spoke to the Spaniard in broken English. "He has gold in the chest he wants to give you. He wants to keep the chest and the girl." The Spaniard did not respond. Akira tried again in mangled Spanish. This brought a look of surprise to the Spaniard's eyes.

"What does he want in return?"

Akira turned to the samurai. "What do you want?"

"Guns."

An hour later Akira's ruse had failed. Not only was the gold loaded onto a longboat for the short row to the galleon, but the chest, Ina, Ono, and Akira as well.

"Where did you learn other tongues?" The Spaniard asked him.

"You wouldn't believe what those Jesuits will teach anyone who will listen."

"That is true of missionaries, my friend. Still, your translation cost you your freedom."

"I would not have left her," he responded.

"You wouldn't have had a choice. So, perhaps, you got what you wanted. We will discuss the offer you made me on the way to the ship, before we meet the captain. Until then, and after then, silence."

"Yes."

Spanish sailors moved to push the longboat to sea. The young samurai approached while his retinue loaded crates of blunderbusses into the back of Ina's wagon.

"Thank you, princess. I understand you are to enjoy your voyage unmolested. You are to be a gift to a king, which may not be to your liking, but I wager is far better than being a gift to a sailor, or the sea."

"Perhaps. Perhaps not." Ina's fingers again found the blade concealed in her kimono, and again hesitated. She might need it later. Revenge is not a good enough reason to lose your weapon. But it was not her only weapon.

Ina's hands shot out, still bound, and the samurai ducked and cringed in surprise, protecting his good eye. Ina only had the reach to dig her fingers into its yellowed brother, and she ripped it from its socket as the samurai howled in pain and rage. Blood spattered across her face as she held the eye aloft. The warrior roared again, and jammed a glove into the seeping socket as he advanced. The Spanish sailors blocked his path and the Spaniard's chuckles drifted across the water.

"Guess I'll have to keep an eye on her," he said as his men erupted in laughter.

Ina held the eye in her fist, crushing it slowly, and the wet popping sound found the samurai's ears along with her words.

"I curse you and I curse this place. This blood poisons this sand and this sea. You have angered the gods, and blood will have its way out and find revenge." She flung the mangled eye into the waves where it drifted away from shore and sank. No fish would touch it as it spiraled down, down to the sandy bottom. There it was covered with silt and began to drain the last of its blood deep into cracks in the earth.

On the Way to Ship

Elbow's dive boat was as grizzled as its owner. A small, squat, proud vessel, it carried Mercy gently in the bow as he piloted from a center console. The six feet of deck behind Elbows found itself stacked neatly with dive gear, tanks secured to gunwales, scuba rigs already attached, valves off so no air leaked. An underwater metal detector lay flat on the deck. It resembled its land based counterparts, only with substantially more attitude.

Mercy enjoyed the wind of the open bow in her hair, and didn't understand why so much money was spent on big, enclosed vessels. If somebody wants a living room, she thought, why don't they stay at home? She did not ignore the fear gnawing at her, but simultaneously refused to let it take charge. She allowed the events of her last dive to play out in her mind a final time, but distantly, like watching a fight on TV from the other side of a large room.

"I'm not trying to rub anything in, but no Alex?" Elbows asked.

"He didn't come home again. As the kids say, I'm over it. It's really time for me to move on, Elbows. That's why I let you talk me into this. It's time to close the circle and move on. It just takes a little push in the right direction."

"What do you think he's up to?"

"Don't know, don't care. The last time I tried to talk to him he said something about a get rich quick scheme with Jack Sweet."

"Holy shit. Kenny." Elbows shook his head and adjusted the boat's course down the coast. Ship Rock loomed in the distance.

"Who's that?"

"Not sure. Pretty sure that's not his real name, just his island moniker, as it were. A couple of years ago, in fact, about the time... Sorry."

"Hey, I said today was about closing the circle. What happened?"

"This guy was in the bar talking shit about Jack Sweet. Now, like him or not, nobody questions the fact that the man can fly. And that's precisely what this guy Kenny was doing."

"Why?" Mercy asked.

"He was looking for the best pilot he could find. He was also testing Sweet's temperament, and his character. He wanted somebody good, somebody with a bit of a temper, and somebody he could talk into making a smuggling run."

"That's how you make half a million bucks in a day." She laughed.

"Alex?"

"Yes. I wonder why he even bothered to try to tell me."

"I've known for years how easy it would be to fly something unsavory to the island. Smart money would hide it here for awhile before boating it to the mainland."

"And what better place to hide something than underwater."

"Big risk."

"Depends on how much you have to lose, I guess." Mercy watched Ship Rock grow larger as Elbows motored towards it.

Elbows pulled two bottles of water from the small cooler next to the center console and passed one forward to Mercy. "I wonder what happened," he mused.

"I'll tell you exactly what happened. Alex hung around as long as it suited him. He never wanted to talk about what happened, he never acted like he saw a happy ending to anything other than our bottles and his massages, and when he had an opportunity to get rich, to hell with the legality, risk, relationship, everything, it was fuck or walk, pal. That's what happened."

"Looks like it." Elbows slugged his water. "What I meant was, what happened to the *Content*? If that's where your coin came from. How did she end up this far north, and what sent her to the bottom? What the hell happened to that ship and what was on it?"

Escape

Ina awoke from her dream with a start. She lay tucked into the corner of the prisoner's hold of the *Content* and found Akira and Ono staring at her forlornly.

"I know of what you dreamt," Akira whispered. "I am sorry we could not save you."

"You did save me. You protected me from the Spanish. And the Japanese. You protected the chest. You even bribed the Spaniard to hide it separately from the rest of the treasure."

Ono blushed. "Well, perhaps not bribe, exactly…"

"You did bribe him!" Ina said. Akira smiled.

"True. I also, ah, encouraged him to think he could sneak it away himself when we reached Spain, rather than turn it over to the king."

Ina pressed her lips together. "Greed is a powerful thing."

"But there is no bribing this one. He has already deserted his companions. He wants everything for himself. The ship, the treasure, you. I will kill him first." Akira stood and grasped the bars of the hold. Ono rose a put a hand on his shoulder.

"No one doubts your bravery, my friend. But we are out of options. We cannot even protect her now."

"Enough. We will tolerate this no longer." Ina slipped the dagger from the folds of her kimono and slid it into the lock on the cell door. Ono crouched beside her.

"It's not worth it. You should wait. We have nowhere to go. There is nothing out there but water and wilderness."

The shackles holding Ina to the chest scraped softly together as she laid her hands on it. "I have no faith in that man. I only told him of this for two reasons. First, it is too beautiful and too important to leave beneath that hollow wreck for the Spaniards to plunder. And, it was worthless to us if we allowed ourselves to be taken without it. Now, at least we have his attention."

Akira placed a hand atop one of the shackles. It shook slightly. "Even if we escape, where do we go?"

"We trust in nature. I have more faith in her than all these men combined. There will be an answer. There always is an answer. We can trade, we can barter, we can pray, we can hope, we can have faith in ourselves." With the briefest click of protest the cell door groaned and swung open.

Ono started. "Where did you learn to do that?"

"The duties of a lady in training are many, as are the uses of a good kaiken." Ina smiled at her friend and began to work the shackles on her left wrist with the knife tip. The sound of bootsteps filtered down from above.

"They change the guard for the last time tonight. We are running out of time," Akira said. As if in response, the shackle snapped open.

"Yes, a little faith. One more, princess."

Ina twisted the bone handle in her right hand, trying futiley to work the tip into the shackle key hole on the same wrist. A look of concern crept across her face as she shifted the kaiken to her left hand. The remaining shackle stared back stubbornly, and the deck tilted beneath them. The chest slid against the port wall, pulling Ina with it, as the vessel turned to the left.

Akira held the bars to steady himself. "We are tacking to sea. Our chance is lost. To abandon ship in the open ocean is certain death. We need land close by."

"Perhaps it is just that the shoreline curves. We are not far away," Ono offered hollowly.

Ina continued to work with stubborn insistence on the right shackle. Slowly a placid look returned to her face and the knife fell still. "I'm not supposed to abandon it."

Akira, exhausted patience evident in his voice, said, "We must decide now. If there is no shore in sight when we reach the deck, we are lost."

"Let's go back in our cell. Close the door. Wait." Ono's voice still rang hollow in the hold.

"No, Akira is right. We must go now."

"But you are still chained."

"We bring it with us. This is as it should be. Even if the shackle yielded, we would bring it with. For centuries we guarded this from the bandits, from the thieves. Chinese, Japanese, Portugese. The pirates do not get this. Not the Spanish pirates, not the English. Things such as this are for those with honor."

Silenced, the men struggled to lift the chest. The ship tilted to port again, staggering them against the bulkhead. Akira growled under his breath. "We are turning again."

"Come on, quickly. Now is the time for strength." Ina wedged her shoulder under the chest as the men heaved, and it scraped up the wall and clear of the floor.

She rolled her chains into the slack of her kimono, silencing the clinking as best she could. Akira and Ono flanked her, the chest between their straining arms, and the three moved from the hold as quickly and quietly as their awkward formation would allow.

Airport in the Sky

Alex drove an ancient primer gray Chevy Blazer up the narrow dirt road out of town, through the gate that allowed only locals and those with permits into the interior of the island, and clawed up the steep slope towards the Airport in the Sky. Some half a century earlier, the Wrigley family carved out an airstrip atop a flat hill in the rugged interior. Barely large enough to handle the DC-3 responsible for bringing the mail, the runway sat off-camber, with a cliff like drop into canyons on either end and jagged hills overlooking all. Frequented almost exclusively by experienced sport pilots and transports bringing the rich who didn't like boats, it existed as a throwback to an earlier age of aviation.

"Right on time," the Señora smiled.

"What's he flying in?"

"Sweet decided on a simple Jabiru 170. It's fully loaded with fuel and our packages, but still has the necessary range. He's been at ten thousand feet for the past few hours, conserving fuel and making his way leisurely in. He'll have to refuel once he lands, but we will be on our way back down this hill with our goodies by then."

"Are you coming with me to make the dive?"

"I can't stand the ocean. If it were up to me I'd wait at the hotel, but Kenny wants me to ride along with you."

"Did he say why?"

"Of course. He's worried about you."

The Blazer made the last turn in the road, and the airport lay before them. An old white control tower held a single operator who stood outside on a small wooden balcony, smoking a cigarette and listening for air traffic on his radios. Alex backed the truck into a dirt lot adjacent to the runway and killed the engine. It was still cooling and ticking when they heard the plane. The Señora spotted it first, on approach from the south. Sweet made two more legs of approach, and set the red and white Jabiru down gently, using the dirt next to the tired pavement of the runway to save his tires. He taxied to the edge of the lot as the Señora mounted the steps of the tower to say hello to the controller.

"Lo, Alex," said Sweet as he clambered from the plane.

"Hello, Jack Sweet."

"How's your back?" Sweet opened the plane's cargo door. Alex looked up at the control tower as he opened the back of the Blazer. The controller was inside, showing the Señora the radios. In five minutes a dozen plain brown packages the size of generous Christmas presents transferred from the Jabiru to the Blazer.

"I almost didn't get off the goddamn ground with all that weight and full fuel tanks," Sweet mused. "That would've been one expensive bonfire. I'm going to refuel and get the hell out of here. Pull over to the other side of the lot and wait for your date."

Alex shook Sweet's hand and did as he was told. Jack Sweet fired the Jabiru and taxied to the refueling station. The Señora kissed the controller on the cheek, and made her way down the tower stairs and into the Blazer. Sweet fueled his plane and watched the Blazer kick up dust until it disappeared down the hill.

Back in the Water

Mercy descended slowly into the sea. The sensation was strange, a mix of the rust of not diving in months comingled with the comfort of having dived thousands of times before. Everything was new, and everything was exactly the same. She had finished replaying the events of her last dive for the last time, and left them on the boat above. The pinnacle that was Ship Rock lay in front, reaching up to and beyond the surface, and plunging into the depths below. Mercy looked over and saw Elbows watching her calmly. His ancient scuba rig looked like the prop trucks for Sea Hunt and the Cousteau videos had been involved in a nasty accident. In addition to the metal detector he carried wire cutters, chisels, a backup air tank, and lift bags rolled tightly and secured to his rig. His white hair waved in the water like some seaweed covered mythological beast, and Mercy laughed despite herself. Her grin broke the seal on her mask and it flooded. She simply took a deep breath, pressed the mask against her face, tilted her head back, and blew air out her nose, filling her mask and forcing the water out. She winked at Elbows and they continued their slow descent towards the terraced drop off.

When the edge of the pinnacle approached, Elbows activated the metal detector and began to play it over the bottom. Mercy noted their depth at sixty feet as they began a search pattern along the scalloped terrain of the rock. When she was certain they had covered the ground from which the boy had bolted, they dropped a bit deeper and reversed direction. Two tank changes and two hours later they continued the same sweep. Twice the detector pinged. Once they were rewarded with a bottle cap, once with a cell phone. Elbows flipped it open and pushed it to his ear, then held it out to Mercy. He took his regulator out and mouthed, "It's for you." Mercy flooded her mask laughing again, and they continued their search.

Two more passes on the pinnacle later, Elbow's metal detector pinged again, much stronger this time. He hovered above a rocky substrate, a tangle of rocks and clay and kelp and what might have once been coral in a warmer sea. Elbows handed Mercy a short pry bar, and she began to chip away at the bottom. Kelp holdfasts broke away first, the billowing plants drifting away in a slight current.

Mercy continued to chip away at the mass, and with a strike of the pry bar, the corner of a chest became visible. She turned and looked at Elbows, who nodded and gestured for her to check her air. She glanced at her gauges, flashed him an "ok" sign and continued to work. Her pulse quickened in her chest and her fingers, and she forced herself to breathe slow and deep.

Mercy chipped away the length and height of the chest. A bottom corner revealed itself, and a damaged fitting allowed a coin to fall out. By some trick of the water, it appeared to glow.

"This is it, they're the same," she whispered into her regulator as she peered at the coin. "But that's not all that's in there. What is that light?" She turned the coin over in her hand and then handed it to Elbows. He nodded to her and gestured back to the chest. She continued to chip away.

Mercy slowed her pace further, taking her time around the top of the chest. As the encrustations fell away, a dagger revealed itself sunk deep into the chest's lid. It showed no corrosion whatsoever. A faint luminescence shone from the line where the knife disappeared into the chest.

Castoff

Ina, Akira, and Ono reached the deck and slipped along the gunwale of the *Content*. A sliver of moonlight illuminated their furtive movements dimly, and twinkled down on a deserted shoreline and a rapidly growing expanse of black sea as the vessel turned for open water. The Engilsh kept a light watch, and those few sailors on duty peered to stern, knowing full well the penalty for mutiny should Cavendish and the *Desire* overtake them.

The prisoners crouched underneath a long boat. It was still wet from its foray with the *Santa Ana*, and cold drops of salt water dripped onto Ina's raven hair and the stubbled, bald skin of the men. Their eyes met briefly, Ina nodded, and the men stepped from beneath and heaved the chest up and into the boat, letting it slide inside. It rocked on its ropes and pullies, and Akira pressed his shoulder against it to still it. Ina pulled herself up, over, and inside. As she settled in next to the chest the open shackle slipped from her gown and clanked against the hull of the longboat. Footsteps approached from the stern, and Akira and Ono crouched again in the shadows underneath the boat.

"What are you doing, Bernardo?" The guard's voice drifted across the deck of the *Content* to the hiding men.

"I thought I heard something."

"The whole damn crew is spooked."

"Not me. I'm doin' my duty."

"Like hell. The reason we're spooked is we're not doing our duty. We're mutineers."

"Prove it. We got lost in the fog."

"Maybe."

"I know I'm not as spooked as I was angry when Admiral Cavendish took all the treasure."

"He didn't take all of it."

"Hmm?"

"You honestly think our Captain would've 'gotten lost in the fog' if we didn't have something to show for it?"

"I thought the plan was to take more Spanish vessels with Cavendish, and sail home the long way around."

"Bernardo, how long have we been out here?"

"Two years. Two bloody years with no gold, no women, for us anyway, nothing."

"How many ships, I mean treasure galleons, have we taken?"

"You know as well as I."

"Right. One. How much treasure did we get?"

"It looked like a King's ransom to me."

"That's not what I asked you."

"Huh?"

"How much treasure did *we* get?"

"Right."

"We can chase the Spanish bastards as well as Cavendish. Maybe better. And now we get to keep what we get. And, on top of that, we're not starting from scratch."

"What do you mean?"

Ina crouched in the longboat, listening to the guards, trying not to shake her chains with her trembling. Akira and Ono flattened themselves underneath the suspended boat, staring at the guards' boots to stern.

"You didn't see the Captain go back ashore with the Oriental prisoners."

"No, Francisco. I didn't. Why would he? Did he release them?"

"No. He brought them back. And he brought something back with them."

"Really..."

"It's locked in the prisoner's hold with them."

"Why there?"

"Only the Captain and the Navigator have access. I take care of the Navigator's extra grog. I'll have him show you in the morning."

"And when we get home?"

"Well, damn if we didn't get lost in the fog and just had to think for ourselves, and get rich in the process."

"And Admiral Cavendish and the men on the *Desire* know nothing of whatever came aboard?"

"If he suspected anything, he wouldn't have been so far out to sea. He never would've let us out of his sight. You saw how he handled the haul from the galleon."

"Right."

"Come on. We're rich and getting richer, thanks to Captain Edmund. Time for some of that grog. We're the most dangerous thing out here."

"Lead on, sir. Lead on."

From beneath the longboat Akira and Ono could see the guard's boots turn and retreat. When they had disappeared, the men rose and peered in at Ina. Ono looked at his friend.

"How are we going to lower the boat and get aboard?"

Akira lips curled in a tight smile. "We will manage. Come on, into the water."

Ina poked her head up and out of the longboat. "Wait, once the boat is in the water you won't be able-"

"Quiet, princess. We knew we weren't coming along. We will return to the cell and hide your disappearance as long as we can."

If there is such a thing as a glare of love, that was what Ina leveled at Akira. Ono peered across the deserted deck of the *Content* and then grabbed the hemp line beneath the pulley at the bow of the longboat. Akira moved to the stern. Without a word, they pushed the longboat out into space and lowered it into the dark water. It bobbed alongside, bumping gently into the English ship.

Ono played out more line. "Quickly. Someone will hear."

"Cast off princess. You are a prisoner no longer," said Akira.

"Farewell my friends. We will meet again, here or elsewhere." Ina grabbed an oar with her free hand and used it to push the longboat away from the *Content*. The other oar dipped into the water beneath her shackled hand. She fixed a placid gaze up at the faces of Akira and Ono, and rowed away into the night.

Mercy of the Elements

Jack Sweet finished fueling his plane, climbed inside, and began to taxi back to the turnaround, planning his takeoff. He was about to pivot the Jabiru onto the tarmac when the whine of an engine and a tremendous cloud of dust caught his eye. The Blazer roared back into sight, bounced across the airport entrance, and tore across the dirt parking lot towards him. For a moment he thought that it meant to ram him, then Alex stood on the brakes and spun the wheel, bringing the Blazer to a halt next to the plane. An enormous dust cloud engulfed them as Sweet leapt from the cockpit, leaving the engine idling.

"What the fuck?!"

"Cops, cops!" Alex yelled over the engine. The Señora jumped from the truck. "Get us the hell out of here!" Alex moved towards the plane, stopping only when he saw the revolver in Sweet's hand.

"I'd love to, son, but if we abandon the merchandise we're all dead. You think Kenny can't find you? Now, re-load the plane. I'll get the packages out of here. You keep your mouths shut and all they'll have you on is suspicion. You might sweat a bit of time, but Kenny will take care of you when you're out, if you keep quiet."

"Goddamn you, Sweet!"

159

"Alex, he's right. Come on, help me." The Señora moved to the back of the Blazer and began lugging a package towards the Jabiru. The din of sirens crept into the dust cloud as it began to settle and the sound to rise.

"Move, kid." Sweet had a package in his arms and carried it towards the plane. Alex cursed again and grabbed a box himself. The controller stood at the railing of the tower, speaking into his cell phone and pointing.

As Alex moved towards the Jabiru with the last box, two police units burst into view. The off road vehicles looked like miniature humvees, and their flashing lights and sirens cried doom from the opposite side of the parking lot. Another dust cloud chased the cops towards the plane. The Señora glared in defiance and began to walk towards the police.

"Come on, Alex. Get Sweet out of here, and keep your mouth shut. When they say, 'you have the right to remain silent,' do it."

Sweet crawled into the cockpit. He heard Alex slam the cargo door and he gunned the engine. The Jabiru responded, pulling away from the onrushing cops. The tower squawked into his headset and he ignored the orders to stop. He spun the plane at the edge of the runway, and buried the throttle. The Jabiru bucked and began to race down the tarmac.

Halfway down the runway, Sweet checked his speed. He did not have enough to take off. He jammed the throttle again and rapped the airspeed indicator with his knuckles. "Come on, goddamn it, I know we're full but we've got the horsepower." Another hundred meters down the runway he had his speed.

"This is gonna be close," he whispered as he yanked back on the yoke and the plane began to climb. Then he heard a thump from the back. As the wheels struggled to leave the earth, Sweet pivoted his head to see Alex crouched behind him, his body crammed in between the packages. Sweet's face froze as he realized they were overweighted. Alex saw his expression, and a moment later Sweet saw his frozen stare on Alex's face. Jack Sweet spun his head back around just in time to see the runway disappear beneath them as the plane screamed in protest.

From his vantage point outside the tower, as the controller told it later, it was not so much as if the plane fell to the ground, as the earth had rose up and swatted it from the sky. A fireball engulfed the Jabiru as it ceased to be. Flames spread quickly to the surrounding hills and a smoke as black and thick as sackcloth rose into the still air.

-

The sun broke above a shoreline clear and cold and much too far away. Ina smiled sadly, her face etched with fatigue. Each stroke of the oars carried her farther away from the *Content*, yet despite angling sharply for land, a stubborn breeze pushed her farther and farther to sea. Occasionally she glanced over her shoulder, watching the land move slowly by but no closer. With each stroke of the oars the chains on her right wrist scraped along the bottom of the longboat. The chest sat behind her, between her and the bow of the boat, and her back brushed against it each time she finished the oars' stroke.

After another hours' rowing, this time in the light of a new day, Ina began to sing softly. Not even the small waves could hear her words, but the wind caught them and carried them to port, away from land. She turned and looked after them, and there, on the opposite side of the boat, land appeared. For a moment she believed that she had become disoriented in her exhaustion, and was somehow rowing back towards the *Content* rather than north. A check over her left shoulder revealed this not to be the case. In the light of the clear day she could see land on both sides. To her left, the east, the sun glared down on the mainland, at least twenty miles distant. She could not see the shore itself, but a low line of hills, a sea bluff, and much higher mountains behind. Snow kissed the tops of the tallest. To her right, the west, a stout chunk of island thrust from the water, no more than a few miles away.

"Perhaps the winds have decided for me," she said to the water, and pulled harder with the starboard oar until the longboat pointed directly at the island. Then she bent to rowing again, her back brushing the chest and the island growing closer with each stroke.

It was the rays of the rising sun striking the *Content*'s sail that caught Ina's eyes. The white glare reflected across the water, bridging the miles of ocean between them in an instant, and burning into her widening stare. She feared for her companions. What had the English Captain done to them when he discovered her missing? What would he do to her should he overtake her? And the chest? She redoubled her efforts at the oars, willing the island closer to her. It was maddening to have it behind her, to stare at the sail growing steadily closer as the *Content* ran down its prey. To check her progress she was forced to twist and stare over her shoulder, and this did nothing for her speed. She did it only often enough to stay on course, and dug the rough wood of the oars into the water and into her palms with each stroke. Still the *Content* drew nearer.

The chop of the channel water calmed and Ina found herself in the wind-shadow of the island. Her hands throbbed from the rowing, yet each time her back touched the chest the muscle aches disappeared. She rowed until the small skiff floated underneath a steep hillside, next to a pebbled beach. She lifted her eyes to the approaching *Content*. The entire vessel was now easily visible beneath its sail, and growing steadily larger. Keeping her eyes on the craft, she withdrew her dagger from her kimono and set to work on the shackle once more. Again, her left hand betrayed her. Again, she tried to hold the kaiken in her right hand and pick the shackle on the same wrist. Again the lock would not yield. Then the light wave action beached the boat.

Ina scrambled from the longboat and into knee deep water. It soaked her gown and whirled around her ankles, cool but not cold. The gentle swell pushed the keel of the boat onto the pebbly beach, the rattle of stones in the surf both welcoming and warning her. She turned and grasped the chest, attempting to lurch it out and let the boat float free. It refused to budge. A low growl crept from between her teeth as she set her slippered feet in the rocky bottom and heaved again. Still nothing. A larger swell lifted and floated the boat before pulling it back to sea. The chain grew taut and dragged Ina, still growling, into the surf. She grabbed the chain and used it to haul herself back onboard.

"As you wish," she said to the chest. Ina grabbed the oars again, startled at how much closer the *Content* had drawn during her struggle in the surf. She set her back to rowing, and fled from Edmund and the English down the length of the island.

Hours later, the *Content* finally bore down on her. A natural bay and then a curve in the island drew the shoreline away from Ina as she continued rowing roughly north, and she found herself perhaps a hundred yards offshore but still paralleling it. A rocky pinnacle rose from the depths and cast its shadow over her shoulder as she approached it. She ignored the *Content* and continued to row as the vessel overtook her and pulled along side. Edmund appeared at the port rail.

"Give it up. There is nowhere to go." He swept his hands wide to indicate the futility of her actions. "Nowhere. Nothing! Are you going to make this easy for me, or fun?" Sailors began to gather around the railing of the *Content*, smiling as they had when the *Santa Ana* galleon came within range. Ina began to sing softly to herself and continued to row.

"Lower a net!" bellowed Edmund. The crew snapped to and soon a net slithered down the side of the *Content*. A boarding party of sailors armed themselves with pistols and cutlasses and scrambled to the net.

"No. She's caused enough trouble. I'll handle this myself." The men cheered their captain, the man brave enough to defy Cavendish. They saw the chest now, and the girl chained to it, and their hero regaining what was lost - not once, but twice. The blood coursed through their veins and they felt the pride of privateering and the dark thrill and joy of piracy.

Edmund made his way to the net and began to climb down. Ina continued to row, her eyes locked on Edmund's back. The *Content* banged into the longboat. Ina was thrown against the port oar and she cried out as it forced the air from her lungs. The chest pitched and tilted against the forward gunwale, and the chains rattled against the planks.

Edmund held fast to the net as it swung from the impact, and glared over his shoulder at Ina. "Brave, but stupid. I've no more patience with you." He leapt the few remaining feet into the longboat. Edmund landed with a heavy thud, but rose and spun easily to face Ina. Still she continued to row.

"You're not scared. You will be."

As Edmund reached for her, Ina's kaiken flashed from her kimono, the steel slicing across his torso and plunging for his neck as if it could smell the blood there, just beneath the thin skin. The chain snapped tight, stopping the blade a hand's width from the artery. Edmund screamed in pain and rage and grabbed her shackled wrist. Ina refused to let go of the dagger, and twisted to free herself from his grasp as a thin red line began spreading across his tunic.

Edmund slammed Ina's wrist against the longboat's plank bench, sending the knife clattering to the deck. She reached for it with her free hand, but the Englishman was faster. The kaiken grew cold in his hand, to the point of discomfort, but he ignored the numbness and held the blade underneath Ina's throat. She gazed up at him calmly. Edmund laughed at her stoicism, raised the dagger above her head, and slashed it downward, slamming it into the wood of the chest behind her. The thwock of metal meeting wood reverberated throughout the boat, and still Ina did not flinch. Edmund shook his head and laughed again.

He grabbed Ina's throat and pressed his grizzled cheek against hers. "I am going to break you. And then I am going to kill you."

The sound of steel snapping shut sent a wave of disbelief over Edmund's face. He looked down to see the loose shackle clamped around his wrist. He tightened the grip on her throat as he stared at the shackle.

"You think I don't have the key?" Edmund pointed to his pocket with his free hand.

Now Ina smiled at him. A strange, sad, smile of acceptance of the beauty and the ugliness in the world. "No," she said in formal Japanese, "and you never will." Ina reclined back against the tilted chest, and drove a kick into Edmund's chest. It landed with the dull thud of a bullet striking flesh, and spilled Edmund onto his back. The chain rattled after him, snaking to the shackle on his wrist. Ina wedged her shoulder under the tilted chest and pushed it, scraping, up the side of the longboat and onto the rail. It began to teeter in the breeze and the swell.

"No!" The men on the *Content* screamed. Some began climbing down the net. Others drew their weapons and fired at Ina. Shooting down such a steep angle, the sailors failed to compensate, and the lead balls flew high, splashing the water behind her. As they paused to reload, Edmund scrambled to his knees and grabbed the chain, dragging himself towards her.

Ina gave him a sad, dismissive glance, looked to the sky, and pushed the chest into the water. The chains hissed over the edge as Edmund's eyes grew wide. Then the chains snapped tight and dragged both Edmund and Ina overboard and into the sea.

Edmund thrashed against the shackle as the chest plunged for the bottom, invisible in the depths beneath them. A rush of bubbles escaped and raced back for the surface as a pale light glowed from within. Ina stretched her arms out calmly, her kimono fluttering like a new fledged dove as she disappeared into the depths.

-

Elbows backed away and watched as Mercy chipped the last of the substrate from the chest. The rusted remains of a shackle fell away with the final piece. Mercy tucked the dagger into a vest pocket, and Elbows handed her a lift bag. She unrolled the bag and clipped two lengths of line to each handle of the chest. She used her alternate regulator to blow air into the open bottom of the lift bag. It inflated and floated for the surface. The lines grew tight and the buoyant bag eased the chest from its grave.

Mercy held the chest to hers, and began to kick gently upwards towards the air and the light. When she reached the surface, it would be time to look inside.

Acknowledgments

The author wishes to gratefully acknowledge the encouragement, critique, sharp eyes, and warm hearts of:

Peter Bricklebank

Mike Carter

Anaya Jones

Amber Mandler

Scott Patterson

John Seery

Donna Sharpe

Connor Walker

and

Andi Scarbrough, my sweet love.

About the Author

Christopher Blehm, BA, MFA, teaches both English and scuba diving. He has lived and worked in Colorado, the Bahamas, on Grand Cayman, and in Europe and Egypt. He currently divides his time above and below the water on Catalina Island.

Thank you for reading this book.

Please comment on Amazon.com

facebook at Mercy of the Elements

and mercyoftheelements.com

Made in the USA
Charleston, SC
06 May 2011